THE PLATED HEART

Diane Goodman

Carnegie Mellon University Press
2006

In memory of Betsy Pisanelli, whose great heart is missed by everyone who knew her.

Acknowledgments

All thanks and love to Laurel, Kathie, Jen, Michelle, and Rick, who read these stories and helped me make them better; mostly, to my editor and friend Sharon Dilworth. And to my family for their love and encouragement.

Book Design: Andrew K. Cramer
Type set in Sabon.
Cover Design: Leif Kolt

Library of Congress Control Number: 2005933841
ISBN-13: 978-0-88748-452-0
ISBN-10: 0-88748-452-2
Printed and Bound in the United States of America

10 9 8 7 6 5 4 3 2 1

CONTENTS

You could laugh and cry in a single sound.

Bruce Springsteen, *For You*

The Manager

She was crying as she left the grocery store, mumbling to herself like a homeless woman and crying like a woman whose heart had just been broken. The automatic people mover leading to the parking garage cranked too slowly, up and up and she held on to the grocery cart and clicked her heels as if she was Dorothy and could make herself disappear. She took her glasses off to wipe away the tears that were dark with the eye make-up she'd so carefully applied. She used the bottom of her new sheer shirt to rub it off.

Her car was black and she had had it washed the day before but the sand and dust of the beach had formed a dirty layer already. This seemed sad, too. Irrevocably sad and unfair and she hurled her groceries into the back of the car as if they were sacks of bricks instead of eggs and bottles of oil, vinegar, mayonnaise—things that would shatter. She flung the turkey into her car with the power and purpose of breaking it apart.

At home, things were just as she'd readied them. Table set with flowers, new ceramic candlesticks, linen napkins. A small lamb roast was marinating in the refrigerator, greens in a bowl to be tossed and dressed, strawberries dipped in expensive chocolate. It was New Year's Eve. She lifted a bottle of champagne from a grocery bag, opened it, and took a warm swig.

She was a private chef in Miami Beach and spent her days in a stranger's kitchen and in the grocery store. She spent her nights alone. It had taken some time for being alone to be effortless but now she was good at it: her house was gleaming and impeccably organized; she had books to read when she wasn't cooking and music or television to listen to when she was so there were always distant voices to join or block the voices she knew in her head. She worked for a wealthy family and at their house, she communicated in nods and gestures and smiles with the housekeepers, personal assistants, butler and groundskeeper who only spoke Spanish. She petted the dogs and fed them scraps to keep the pull she felt in her chest when they rested their big bodies against her thighs as she cooked. She had a simple, orderly life. But then things in the grocery store got rough.

She heard him before she saw him the first time, a big hearty laugh that sounded so much like Billy's her head flashed around to see if Billy had materialized himself in the world. But he had not; this laugh came from a man standing in front of the seafood case talking to a customer, an elderly woman in a silk sheath and beret. His arms were folded across his chest and the woman had her crinkly hand on his bicep. He was tall, the woman was short, and he looked down on her with a benevolence she recognized. Then he patted the hand on his arm. The gesture, so spontaneous and authentic, made her own hand tingle.

His eyes stayed in her head all day. They watched her unpack her groceries and put them away. They watched her cooking eggplant parmesan for her boss, drinking a glass of wine, wiping up, flipping through a magazine. They watched her wash and undress and get into bed; then when she closed her own eyes, his were behind them.

In the morning, he was still there. While she packed up food to take to her employer, she tried to know him better. Perhaps he was a store manager because he wore a beautiful pressed shirt and a tie and good pants. Other people who worked in the store wore polos with their names on them, aprons or white coats but he was wearing a dark green shirt, black pants with pleats, and a silk tie. She closed her eyes and tried to see his face more clearly but only his body appeared, his good clothes and his big arms crossed over his wide chest. She could not find his face, but she could still see that he was solid.

The second time she saw him she fell in love with him. He stood at the poultry cooler and she watched him give directions to a stock boy; he had his hand on the boy's shoulder. The boy was small with the wide open face of someone who comes slowly to understanding but at the same time she could tell that he was happy to be held in place by that big open hand. She couldn't look away and a ringing started to take up some space in her head. Sometimes when she did parties for her boss and was rushing around the kitchen crowded

with maids and servers, or sometimes when she
was giving a tip to the valets in her building who
brought her her car, she inadvertently touched or
was touched but it was always accidental.

When the stock boy walked away, he did not.
Instead, he stood in the same place and looked out
at the shoppers in the store. Earlier that morning,
she had read her horoscope in the newspaper and
it said "take chances" so she moved closer until she
was standing just behind him, could see the fine
weave of his shirt, this time a white one. She was so
close to him she could almost feel the fabric on her
bare arms but that was a chance she could not take
so she lifted a package of chicken breasts and was
heading back to her grocery cart when he turned
to her and said hello. Just hello, but it was enough.
Actually, it was too much. She opened her mouth to
say hello back but then found she had to catch her
breath. He smiled and walked away. His eyes were
blue.

Billy's eyes were usually green. Sometimes, in
certain lights or certain clothes, they were hazel or
brown. But always they were lively and welcoming.
Billy was the outgoing one, the one who got the
catering clients, negotiated with the vendors, made
friends and kept them forever. She knew no one
in Miami except her boss's family because after
Billy, she found it difficult to speak. She could not
explain things and meeting people always involved
explanations. That was the beauty of her boss
and her boss's family—they were not interested in
nor curious about her. They did not want to get

to know her beyond the service she provided. She slipped into their house quietly, put the groceries away, prepared and packaged meals their servants would later serve them, and left when she was done. When her boss had a special request, she taped a note to the bulletin board above the phone. Often, weeks would go by without them ever seeing each other and sometimes she wondered if her boss would recognize her if she ran into her on the street.

Hers was a life that demanded very few personal decisions. She wore sweat pants and t-shirts to cook in, to go to the grocery store, to run errands, to sleep. She cooked to live and ate only small amounts of whatever she was preparing for her boss that day. She re-read her old books, watched reruns on television, clipped her hair back with the same barrette every day, had one old swimsuit, a worn pair of sandals, Billy's windbreaker, the plastic coffee mugs they'd won at the Crawford County Fair. Sometimes in day dreams, she still saw her ceramic dishes and wine glasses, her picture frames, her silk dresses and good suits and paperweights and throw pillows and Billy, all whole and safe and packed into the rental truck and whizzing down I-95 from Pennsylvania to Florida. But she learned early on that if she spent too much time seeing the things she loved, the things that belonged to her, then suddenly glass and fabric and feathers and bone would be flying through the air, smashing on the ground, broken, dented and bloody, so she learned to stop, to will the images to pale and thin away.

But after that first hello, things changed. She felt a need to return to the deeper past, the one beneath the few small things she had kept, in order to negotiate the present. She conjured memories she had buried so she could remember what she was supposed to do. She knew Billy knew what was happening, what she was feeling. Instead of only appearing in dreams, Billy started showing up during the day in fits and pieces. She heard his voice in her ear when she drove, singing along to the Oldies station, she felt his hand at the back of her neck while she stirred soup. Sometimes she just leaned backwards to try and fit into him; other times, she came right out and asked him what should happen next. He never answered in the usual ways but the day of the second hello, on her way home from work she found herself pulling into the Burdine's parking lot and going into the store to buy some clothes.

The next morning, she changed out of her sweat pants, took a shower and put on a dark blue button down shirt and a pair of new white pants. She put on earrings and lip gloss, too. She combed her hair, rubbed cream into her hands, sprayed on perfume. Hello.

She was coming around the corner from produce when he appeared at the top of the aisle.

Hello, he said. He was smiling. He had nice teeth.

Hello, she answered.

Finding everything you want? he asked.

I'm not sure what I want, she said because that

was true.

Ok, he said, and he drew out both syllables in such a way that she didn't really know what he meant. But it didn't matter: some exchange of understanding was taking place and not everything had to make sense in words.

There were more hellos after that and each one was increasingly sustaining because with each one came the peace of familiarity. Miami Beach was overly crowded but the distances between people were commonplace and understood. She did not know how to narrow those spaces without Billy. She did not have his kind of eyes. But the grocery store was like a small town, a perfect small town. It was like the building where she lived, where the valets and security officers knew her and they smiled and said hello; it was like her boss's kitchen: these were places where she fit in and knew what to do, where she felt some warmth but forged filaments rather than bonds. Now it was true for the grocery store, too, and it gave her something else to live for as she went from small town to small town to small town.

After the first hellos, she looked for him all the time but there were days when she didn't see him, didn't even know if he was there. Then she would leave the grocery store and while driving to her job, she would convert the disappointment that resembled sadness into the rationalization that everything happened or didn't for a reason. She had learned how to believe in this and as time went by, it made the crashing sounds of doors in

the hall slamming or a jar slipping out of her hands
and smashing on the hard tile floor not sound so
much like smaller versions of what she imagined it
must have sounded like when trucks at high speed
collided.

Fall was the most difficult time, though urban
Miami Beach was not rural Pennsylvania and so it
was easier without all those trees turning colors and
the air getting cool. There were no pumpkin farms
or apple cider stands, no garden to dig up or deer
wandering around the pond. There was always and
only sunshine and the sounds of sirens and horns
honking, an ocean with sea birds. The grocery man
reappeared and she smiled at him and said hello
and for a while everything seemed fine but then
there was a time toward the middle of October,
maybe for about two weeks, that he disappeared
again and she didn't see him once in the twelve
times she went shopping for her boss's food. Twice
during those weeks she went to the store twice in
one day. She wondered if he'd been promoted or
fired, if he was on vacation or had been transferred.
There were a lot of grocery stores in Miami Beach.
He could be anywhere. During this time, when she
got home, she unpacked the groceries and while
she prepared to cook, she found herself trying to
recreate every hello, how his voice sounded—low
and a little gravelly but upbeat, with a lilt. She
hadn't realized it but she had memorized his
clothes—black shirt, grey pants, grey and black tie;
white shirt, blue pants, blue patterned tie. Pink shirt
once with a flowered tie: he could get away with it

because he was tall and strong and could laugh at himself. But no matter how well she could conjure these combinations, they fell slack and crumbled in her imagination; now his body would not appear and fill them. During these empty days, she had to take in long slow rushes of air so she could breathe.

Then, on Halloween, he was back. He floated into her vision like a ghost and as she approached the fresh fish counter, he stopped there and seemed to be counting filets of fish. This time, he smiled and nodded and when she drove to work that day, she studied the image that stayed in her head. Day after day after day through the early weeks of November, that image was made more permanent by numerous sightings of him at the store. She believed that he must have also been always waiting to see if she was coming into the store in the same way that she drove there every day hoping she would see him; the smiles they exchanged convinced her because they possessed certain characteristics she remembered and understood—they were sly, grins almost, satisfied, lengthy. Secret. And it often seemed that he was everywhere she was—at a meat counter, in a freezer section, behind the deli counter when she was waiting in line, sorting out the pork loins while she was looking at pork chops, coming around the corner when she was buying her boss's favorite soap. Although he was careful and subtle and only smiled and said hello, she believed when he saw her he noticed her the way she noticed him because she had gone to so much trouble to dress, apply her make up, fix her hair.

It was more difficult to make sense of the days
where she saw him and felt him seeing her but he
didn't look up to smile or say hello. The first time
this happened, she was so startled and stung that
she walked up and down every aisle in the store
without putting a single thing in her cart. Then
she was afraid to make the circuit again to get
the groceries, so she drove home and called her
boss and claimed she was sick: she would come
tomorrow. The next day, instead of going to her
grocery store, she shopped at the store in her boss's
neighborhood, still trying to decide why he had
not said hello to her. She struggled to put herself in
his place, the way she did with Billy after Billy was
gone when she would wake herself up in the middle
of the night and imagine seeing a loud explosive
light that immediately shuttered into a soundless
darkness. But this was different: she had wanted to
be with Billy at the moment when the lights went
out; with the grocery man, right now at least, she
just wanted to understand.

Putting herself in the grocery man's place within
a world she attended every day was not as hard as
putting herself into the nether world of Billy, which
she could only invent. Perhaps the grocery man was
particularly busy on those days that he didn't say
hello, preoccupied, and could not afford to let her
distract him, as he so often distracted her during the
day while she was trying to follow a recipe or keep
butter from burning, as Billy used to so often return
to distract her when she was trying to force herself
back into sleep. She understood the necessity, the

imperative necessity, of staying on track and then she came to believe that she knew she and the grocery man had something serious in common: each one cherished the importance of work. That discovery helped so much that the next day, she returned to her own store.

But he did not say hello to her that day, either. This time, she did make a second trip through the aisles and when she came upon him again, leaning over the dairy case and apparently organizing packages of cheese by brand, she stopped her cart across from where he was and pretended to be comparing types of olives set up on a display behind him. Her back was to his back and every couple of seconds, she'd look over her shoulder, to see if he saw her, if he would smile and say hello. But he did not turn around. She felt he must feel her presence there, as she had felt his so often; when reaching for a rib roast or a whole chicken for soup, her head would turn as if someone called her name and he would be standing somewhere behind her.

She selected a can of large olives and tried to decide what to do next. Her boss's family had all the cheese they needed and her own refrigerator was already too packed with food she'd bought and could not use, food she'd put in her cart and paid for just so she could prolong her time in the grocery store. She knew that if he did not say hello to her today, she would have to use too much energy to push the dark disappointment away and she needed that energy to cook dinner for her boss, the family. Determined, she looked around while

trying to decide how to proceed. She saw boys in
jeans, women with babies in strollers, women in
tight pants and cropped shirts who looked like they
were trying to see who might be looking at them
and then she saw a trio of men in serious dark gray
suits. She had a revelation. There must be bosses,
important men who truly ran the grocery stores,
and then must have to come and check on how
the managers were doing. She looked from each
anonymous face to the man she already knew was
kind-hearted and solid and sure and now she knew
he was also shrewd; these managers were watching
him and he knew it. Now she knew it too. That was
why he could not talk to her; he had to focus solely
on his job. She felt proud of him: she would not
do anything to compromise his position and when
she turned away and headed toward the check-out
aisle, she was smiling in triumphant complicity.

But that nearly did her in. It was an old feeling
she'd disposed of, forced out like so many feelings
she no longer had any use for, but now it was back
as if it had never been banished. She got dizzy
and turned into the paper goods aisle to stop and
get her breath. Her knees rattled and her heart
was beating too fast and her nerves threatened to
unravel and open the way they had the moment
she learned that when Billy had crossed over the
West Virginia border, he was fast asleep. She had
been asleep then too, on Billy's down coat on the
floor of their new apartment in Miami, dreaming
about where they would hang their pictures and
put up the bookshelves, what their bed would feel

like under their tired bodies after a day of moving,
how quickly their catering business would take
off once Billy got there and made some calls and
then the ringing phone woke her like a woman's
scream and she was screaming, a mass of shivering,
quaking muscles and spiraling nerves that prevented
her from standing or walking or even sitting up
sometimes for months. For a long time, she held on
to the last thing they had done at the same time,
sleep.

She took in a long deep breath, steadied
herself against the grocery cart, closed her eyes
and remembered. She could assume nothing, take
nothing for granted. She knew that. She opened
her eyes, let the breath out, and went to pay for
her boss's groceries. While she had considered for
a moment going up to him and boldly saying hello,
she had not and that had saved him from making
a mistake in front of people who could judge him.
She had saved him. She was glad, grateful, to do
it but she would not think of it as something they
had done together. She would think of it as what
it was: something she had done alone for someone
else. That was so much better, like shopping and
cooking.

But a few days later, she was in the checkout
line when she heard his voice and turned to see
him standing at the bottom of the aisle behind her,
talking to another man in a shirt and tie. She drove
to work in a kind of rejuvenation she feared but
sometimes did not know how to extinguish: it used
to come in day and night dreams when suddenly

Billy would appear out of nowhere and start
laughing or singing just to let her know he was still
there. This is what the grocery store man had done:
he had put himself near her and had spoken loudly
so she would turn around and know he was there.
Billy's absence had not been replaced, exactly, but
it had prepared her to register meaning in realms
where he could not appear. There were many ways
to communicate when talking was not an option
but this was better than the proof that came in
dreams; this had happened in the world.

    The shelf-life of these near encounters
was eternal and they grew and morphed like
experiments. She spent long hours alone in her
kitchen cooking for her boss and although she kept
the television on so sounds would fill her small
apartment, she barely heard them for the fictions
in her head. There, the man from the grocery store
was always watching her even if she couldn't see
him. No matter where she was. She believed that
when she was at the store he saw her and his heart
began to race, that he worked in the coolers slowly,
hoping her next stop would be where he was: she
willed their intuitions to pool together so that he
would always know where she was going to be.
In her mind, he watched her from afar, admired
her new clothes, clean nails, sparkly hair clips.
When his shift was over, she projected him driving
around the beach thinking he might see her, figure
out where she lived, stop his car and invite her for
a drink. When she was home, he hovered over her
like a protective apparition.

Even though she knew Billy wanted her to be happy, sometimes he got jealous and appeared pale and evanescent, growing bigger and bigger like a gossamer balloon until there wasn't anymore room in her head for anyone else. Then she would put on a Bruce Springsteen tape and she and Billy's voice would sing along together, remember their plans, how they wanted to name their kids Spanish Johnny and Rosalita, how leaving Pennsylvania was inevitable because they had been born to run. She would play the tape over and over again so that it was never ending. Then Billy was satisfied and knew she'd always love him so he would fade and deflate and the grocery store man would reappear but they would never make plans: they would just eat and drink wine and walk on the beach or go for a swim. They lived in the moment.

Then one day, something actually happened. She was standing at the meat counter looking at various cuts of meat. In a couple of weeks, her boss would be having a big party and she was thinking she should ask someone in the meat department about ordering some tenderloins. She was just about to look up from the meat and try to find someone when he was standing next to her. Normally she felt his presence before she saw him but this time he caught her completely off guard. He was wearing a burgundy shirt and khakis. Her breathing became irregular because something critical was about to take place. He asked if he could help her and she nodded her head but could not break the pause that followed with any words. He asked her if she

needed some meat and she nodded her head again.
He asked her what kind and she pointed to the
tenderloins and he picked one up to hand to her
which caused a surge of anxiety because she had
been to the store so often and had spent so much
money and had so little space left in her refrigerator
that she knew she could not buy the meat now for
a party that was two weeks away so she took a
deep breath, found her voice and said, Not yet and
he said, Sure, and handed her his card—it had his
name and "Store Manager" on it.

She had known it all along: he was a store
manager. And this confirmation then confirmed
everything else: that, and the fact that he had given
her his card—his name and number—brought a full
white calm down on her. It was as simple as that.
She was so sure but while she was being so sure, he
was still talking.

Yeah, give me a call when you're ready and I'll
get your meat, he said.

She smiled.

If I'm still here, he said and he was laughing.

A jolt of panic shot up through her calm and
blasted her smile away. She knew a person could
just disappear. Her eyes got very wide and he must
have worried that he'd upset her because then he
said, Hey, if I win the lottery, I'll be in the Bahamas.
It was a joke. He was joking. She let out a small
sigh of relief. She wanted to say something but
he was backing away from her, backing into a
swinging door that said "Employees Only."

As soon as she got home, she started cooking

whatever could be cooked in her refrigerator so she
could make room for the tenderloins she would
call him to order. She made two dozen pieces of
chicken piccata, broiled lamb chops, made spaghetti
sauce from all the ground beef, minestrone from the
vegetables beginning to rot in the drawer and froze
it all. It had been worth all the trips to the store: she
knew so much more about him now. He was funny.
He liked to make jokes. He had joked around with
her. They were friends.

But she did not need friends; she needed
something more. Each time she went to the store
after that, she wore better outfits, switched from
lip gloss to lipstick, wore higher shoes to make her
legs look shapely, gave up the barrettes and wore
her hair loose and down. There were still some days
when she didn't see him but on the days she did, she
kept him in her view even if it meant lingering over
items she had no intention of buying. She would
inch her way closer to where he was and then she'd
look up with fake surprise and say hello. When
he'd say hello back—sometimes adding how're
you doing? or what's up?—she knew a bond was
growing and that she would not fight it. Then she'd
continue with her shopping and when she was
done, she'd return to all the aisles again, looking
for him but pretending she had forgotten something
and then pretending she had that something in her
cart all along.

There had been a very long time in her life when
enough was enough, when everything she knew
and everything she had was like a huge concrete

wall she was relieved to reach and rest against.
After Billy and until the grocery man, she did not
want anything to upset her routine. But now a new
twitchy impatience was taking over. She needed
to know more about him but didn't know how to
get what she needed. She wanted to talk to him, to
ask him what he did in the evenings, what kind of
music he liked, if he went to the movies, if he'd ever
been married, if he drank coffee or tea or cooked
his own meals, what he liked to read. But she could
not just start a conversation of that magnitude in
the grocery store. And she did not have the courage
to ask him to meet her somewhere else. But then she
remembered he had given her his card: she could
talk on the phone. And she had the perfect ruse
because she needed to order some meat.

A week before her boss's big party, late in the
afternoon when she surmised that his shift was
nearly over and he might have some free time, she
poured a glass of wine, set her notepad with all her
questions printed neatly in front of her, picked up
the phone and dialed.

She navigated through the automatic voice
system to what she assumed was his office, plush
and elegant with leather chairs and a small jar on
his desk filled with hard candy. A woman answered
saying Customer Service and behind the woman's
voice were many other voices, nearly drowning the
woman out. She cleared her own voice and asked
for him. The woman said he was not there. He was
on vacation. For how long? The woman didn't
know. She hung up.

Where would someone like him go on vacation? The mountains? Golfing? A cruise. And with whom? He had made a joke about going to the Bahamas but was it a joke? Was he in the Bahamas with sultry dark island girls? She and Billy had taken little vacations all throughout the year, to the ski resorts in October to watch leaves turn on the mountain trees, camping on the Maryland shore in June; once in February, they drove to Vermont where a freakishly hot sun was shining and the ice on Lake Champlain was melting but on the way home, they got caught in a massive snow storm and spent the night in a hotel in Albany. They lit the paper log in the fireplace, ordered room service and stayed up all night eating shrimp and watching movies. And even though they had planned to wake up at 5:00 and get an early start home, they had slept until 9:00 and then stayed in the hotel bed for many hours after that.

The next day she went to the store and ordered the meat for her boss's party in person, from a woman behind the customer service counter. She made the rounds of the store twice even though she knew he wasn't there. His known absence, while unexpected and upsetting, did make her focus more on her work though, which was good because Thanksgiving was coming up and her boss was expecting out of town guests who were staying several days. Her boss did not like to think about food and so let her make all the menu decisions and that meant she could create dishes based on all the groceries she had at home, things had she bought just so she could linger and plot at the store.

The day before Thanksgiving, she was in the checkout line having not seen him for some time when suddenly she looked up and he was coming toward her. She felt a mad rush of relief and was glad she had a cart full of food because it would take a long time to ring up and she could watch him while she waited. All the groceries in her cart were for her boss's full house and she had to go home and start preparing their holiday meal but she actually had Thanksgiving Day off. He walked up to her, looked into her cart and said, Looks like you'll be cooking for an army and she nodded her head but when he walked away, she panicked: he probably thought she was cooking Thanksgiving for her own family, her own big family from the amount of groceries in her cart, instead of making the entire meal for her boss but then spending her own Thanksgiving Day eating macaroni and cheese in front of the tv. She wanted the grocery man to know that she was free and she wanted to know what he was doing for Thanksgiving and vowed she would ask him what he did the very next time she saw him.

But then, unbelievably, an entire month went by and she didn't see him at all. She went to the store at different times of the day, thinking she was missing him here or there because maybe he had morning meetings or afternoon breaks. Sometimes it was hard to get there when she wanted to because her boss had so many parties during the high season so she would go very early in the morning or even

very late at night, on her way home, because she
speculated that even managers had to change their
regular schedules. But no matter when she went to
the store during that month or how often, she saw
him nowhere. Now her speculations were more
dire because Billy had taken her to the airport the
day she flew down to Miami to rent the apartment
and clean it up so that when he got there, they
could move all their things in and start the catering
business; she had seen him blow her a kiss and
walk away from the gate, to the rental truck full
of everything they owned. In her mind, she saw
him pull onto the highway as her plane pulled up
into the sky and she knew she'd see him in Miami
in three days except after that she only saw him in
dreams or floating in the air around her.

Something was wrong; she could feel it. The
grocery man had already been on vacation so he
couldn't be on vacation now. And she believed that
things between them had grown so much that if he
was in the store, he would take every opportunity
to look for her because she took every opportunity
to look for him, filled her cart with meat and fish
and cheese and vegetables she didn't need and
couldn't afford just in case he might come out
through the "Employees Only" door. She could
not believe that he would risk being transferred to
another store, at least not without telling her. Her
instincts told her something must have happened.
He'd had an accident, an injury, or worse. How
could she find out? She could go to the customer
service department, find the woman who'd taken

her meat order: they had spoken, they had talked.
She would help her. But when she walked over
to customer service, there were several women
working there and although she tried, she could not
remember which woman she had spoken to. She did
not know what to do so she did the only things she
could do: she went shopping as often as she could
and waited.

Christmas came and she spent it making
chateaubriand and roasted vegetables for her
boss and the family. She made bread and salad
with Roquefort and pears. She made a pumpkin
cheesecake and homemade truffles. The next day,
she went to the store to buy ingredients for dishes
her boss could take on the family plane. As she
was coming up an aisle, she saw him ahead in the
seafood department, Her knees got weak: he was
alive and still working at her store. She tried to look
nonchalant but the moment seemed so critical and
she was afraid to miss him again so she moved her
cart very quickly up the aisle. When she got to the
top, he was still standing there, talking to a sushi
chef. She knew he was waiting for her, the sushi
chef a convenient ruse. She said hello.

He asked how her holiday was and she said it
was fine but that she had spent it working.

What do you do? he asked and she told him she
was a private chef.

Then very quickly, as if she'd been waiting to
do it all her life, she asked how his holiday was,
because Billy had told her to act interested in other
people but mostly she did it because she wanted to

know.

Great holiday, he said, I got to spend it with the kids. They had a blast. He was smiling and talking to her but looking around the store, too. That made sense: he wanted to talk to her but he was the manager, he had responsibilities.

Before she could say, Oh, the only word that seemed able to leave her mouth, before she could process the fact that he had kids, he suddenly said, what about tomorrow?

What about tomorrow? In that one question, those three small simple words, all the months of imagined dialogue came together. All the dreaming and wondering and speculating and certainties finally congealed and became solid and real. Tomorrow. She said tomorrow, already thinking about what she would wear, how she would fix her hair, and he said Saturday, you don't have to work on Saturday, do you? and she said, oh, no, I'm free on the weekends and while she waited for him to ask her if she wanted to have dinner or a drink, while she tried to form the words do you want to have dinner or a drink and make them travel from her head to her mouth to the air between them, he said Well, good for you and he put his hand up in the air to "high-five" her. Her heart would have sunk but then it soared because when she put her hand up in return, instead of just slapping her fingers he took her hand and for a single second, he held it.

She cooked a lot of food that day for her boss—hummus and salsa and homemade tortilla

chips, chicken fingers and chocolate cake and
blueberry muffins, tapenade and a goat cheese
torta, all things to sustain and entertain them while
they flew to Europe for a vacation. The whole time
she relived what he had said. He had kids. Was he
married? How could he be? He had taken her hand.
She'd seen him pat stock boys, touch old women
customers, slap other managers on the back but
she'd never seen him take anyone else's hand. He
said he "got to" spend the holiday with his kids so
that must mean he was separated, or even divorced.
She loved kids, had always thought she'd have
some.

On her way to her boss's house the next day
to deliver the food, she stopped at the drugstore
and bought a newspaper so she could read her
horoscope. Billy used to bring the horoscope home
every day and they would read it and then try to
decide if what it said had happened that day. Most
of the time there was something, even if it was
very small, that fit perfectly inside what the stars
predicted. That day her horoscope said, "your
planets are aligned in universal love" and that was
not just something: it was everything. Universal
love meant Billy, too: he was everywhere in the
universe. She needed so little and mined clean what
she needed out of the smallest things. She felt the
pressure of the grocery store man's hand squeezing
hers every minute: her hand on the steering wheel,
in a pot-holder, gripping a wooden spoon—
anywhere her hand was it was warm and then hot
from his touch. It itched. She had a perpetual whirr

in her stomach. He was just about ready to ask
her out but at the last moment, he panicked and
took her hand instead. She understood panic. And
waiting. The hand-hold told her something; it told
her she would not have to wait much longer.

She spent the next week preparing for the
inevitable because the inevitable always happened
and this time she would be ready. Her boss would
not be back until New Year's Day so she had a lot
of time to think. She tried to conjure Billy for advice
but he would not come. At first, that frightened her
but then she decided that his absence was a sign of
his trust in her: she could do this on her own.

On New Year's Eve Day, she read her
horoscope. It said "Travel the road not taken" and
she was happy because she was already halfway
there. By the time she got to the store, having taken
a new route, she was so sure that the grocery man
would be coming over that she had cleaned, set
the table, marinated some lamb. She knew that if
he was still married, he would never have held her
hand. On her way to the meat department to buy a
turkey for her boss for New Year's Day, she picked
up two bottles of good champagne. Seeing them in
the cart fortified her.

She came around the corner and he was wearing
a dark blue shirt and dark gray pants and he
looked so handsome she wanted to touch him.
He was putting packages of chicken wings in the
poultry cooler. She came up near him, cleared her
throat so he would know she was there and said
hello. He looked at her and smiled and said hello.

It was a happy hello and she was sure she detected some relief in it: she was there, on New Year's Eve Day. In her head she heard herself saying what are you doing for New Years Eve? but as soon as she opened her mouth to let the words out, he turned and went back to his work.

She scanned the meat department for regional managers who would be working and spying on New Year's Eve day but didn't see anyone who looked suspicious. She was wearing a brand new lacy grey top and good black shiny pants. She had blown her hair dry, drawn thin dark lines under her eyes, and she was tan from having gone to the beach the previous day. She looked as good as she had ever looked since she'd moved to Miami. Her head started turning itself from side to side because her body refused to move her from that spot and her boss wanted a turkey for New Year's Day but she couldn't find a turkey because suddenly she couldn't see. Shadows started to take up the space in front of her eyes and when she took her glasses off to try and clear them, she thought in a panic that maybe she was blind. She sensed him moving, picking his head up, and then like a real blind person whose other senses could save her, she heard sounds she knew were coming from his voice but her brain was betraying her. She could not understand any of his words.

Excuse me, miss, she finally heard him say, do you need something?

She did need something, after needing so little for so long she needed so much right then. She put her glasses back on and he asked her again but this time in a different way; he said, what do you need? and she heard herself say turkey but in a whisper because the voice didn't know where it was supposed to go and then he pulled a big frozen bird up into the air right in front of her, like magic. Black magic. A dirty trick.

She took it but could not move or speak and just stood there holding it, cold and too heavy, in both of her hands as if it was her heart and staring at him incredulously and he said hey, so you know what to do with that? as if she wouldn't know, as if she wasn't a private chef and hadn't told him so. He raised his eyebrows and she felt her head lower into a single nod but then she couldn't pick it back up and when she didn't move, he said, Well you're in the money now because now she had the turkey she said she needed and motioned that she knew how to cook. But she was still just standing there holding it and then inexplicably he started singing You're in the Money and laughing uncomfortably which was the first time she had seen him be anything but confident and sure and then she knew he was only human.

It was the only thing that made any sense to her because he wasn't being himself and was also acting like she was just any customer needing a turkey for the new year and not someone who he'd been saying hello to for months, who'd so often been where she was in this grocery store, who'd taken up all the air in her apartment, her car, her closet, who'd come to her in all of her dreams.

He was acting as if she was not someone who had marinated a lamb for him and bought him champagne, as if she was not the person whose hand he had taken and held for a single solid second just a week before.

He acted like he didn't even know her.

The Caterer

The table was intentionally imbalanced. We were standing, upright with our hands behind our backs, against the dining room wall, waiting for instructions but for several minutes none came. When the last couple finally arrived, the others were already, defiantly, seated. Hal, the hostess's brother-in-law, sat at the head and to his left, all on one side, were his wife Belinda, her sister Claire— who was the hostess—Claire's husband, who was introduced to us as Professor Rick, an older women who we later discovered was Belinda and Claire's mother Louisa, and Louisa's date. On the other side of the table were two empty places, and the last couple filled them.

Half an hour earlier, and an hour past the time the dinner was to be served, Claire, a thin, nervous woman in her early thirties with bright red hair that was cut in an ultra-modern style that didn't suit her face or discomfort at all, had instructed us to put out the butter pats and the baskets of rolls, to pour water in the glasses and then refill the pitchers and leave them on the table. When the last couple took their seats on their side of the table, there was a thick mix of resentment and relief in the air.

The newly arrived woman was full of

apology—she said she was sorry to Claire and
to Belinda and then she turned and told us, the
caterers, that she was sorry too. Claire said to the
man, *You always have to be late, don't you?* and
then there was some nervous laughter. *But we're
worth waiting for, aren't we?* the man said in a tone
that was a good mimic of Claire's voice and he
lifted his water glass and took a few sips. He was
startlingly handsome, rugged as an action hero, and
when he picked up his bread knife to spread butter
on a roll, his confidence seemed offensive and held
all the others at the table quite still.

Claire rose and walked into the kitchen,
motioning for us to follow. It was only Rachel and
Terry and me for this party, a sit-down dinner for
8, and we had been prepped and ready for over an
hour. When we got into the kitchen, Claire took a
deep breath and, running both hands through her
styled hair, apologized for the late arrival of her
uncle and his girlfriend. Neither she, nor her sister
who also appeared to be in her early thirties but had
a softer, more innocent look, seemed much younger
than the man she called their uncle but we had done
a lot of parties where the families made no sense
so we nodded our understanding; then I asked if
she'd like the first course to be served. *In a couple
of minutes,* she said; *maybe you could get them one
drink? Just one.*

The new woman said she would have a glass of
white wine, the man wanted a scotch and looked
as though he could pound back a few. He was the
tapping-the-foot on the floor, tapping fingers on the

back of his girlfriend's chair type, uneasy but trying
to act like he was merely bored. His girlfriend was
a different kind of jittery: her eyes seemed unable to
stop moving from face to face, looking at everyone
opposite her on the other side of the table, as if
something was going to happen here beyond an
elegant dinner for eight.

Something always happens at every dinner party
we do. A guest accidentally spills a glass of red
wine on a white heirloom tablecloth or someone
has an allergic reaction to something we serve. But
the atmosphere in this house was so tense that it
seemed as though something terrible had already
happened.

The uncle and his girlfriend were both in their
forties but she seemed younger: she had a pretty
face and wasn't wearing any make-up, unlike the
sisters and their mother who looked like they'd
had their make-up done for the occasion and were
wearing mascara and blush and different shades of
pastel lipstick. The uncle's girlfriend had a big smile,
warm, but the way it moved from bright to flat and
back to bright again said she wasn't completely sure
what she was supposed to be doing. She thanked
Rachel when she ordered her wine and then sat
back in her chair, as if she was maneuvering herself
into relaxing; you could tell by the way she sat
down and crossed her legs under a long gauzy skirt
but then re-crossed them and then decided to cross
them back again, by the way she pulled the water
glass toward her and then without taking a sip,
pushed it away again. She had green eyes and very

long very curly black hair.

The kitchen was an open one with a large pass-through window to the dining room. This was both good and bad for caterers: good because it made the passing of the plated food easy and meant it would be hot when the servers set it down but bad because they could see us and we could see them so it would be a careful night—no sticking our fingers into sauces, no rolling our eyes. Rachel went to get the drinks while I set up a tray of champagne flutes that I would fill with cold tomato soup. Terry was spreading pesto on parmesan toasts.

The uncle began talking about his business, using it as a reason for the late arrival. *What are you talking about?* the mother at the end of table said. *It's Saturday—you don't work on Saturday—and you knew this dinner was for 7:00.*

Hey, this is Miami, the uncle said, *no one's on time here.* The mother's date laughed but she did not. *Lighten up, Sis,* the uncle said: *we're here.*

The uncle and the mother were sister and brother. The family now made more sense. We were used to solving such mysteries, where observation led to speculation and bit by bit information not meant for us came to us anyway. All private dinners had long lulls while the people were eating and as we were always anxious to leave once a party was finished, we cleaned up as much as we could along the way but while we were rinsing and stacking plates, we made careful observations so we could compare notes later. The secret world of caterers: we're detectives.

I could already tell Claire, the hostess, was the older sister by the way she stood and sat—erect and authoritative—and by the way Belinda slouched a bit and looked at her sister for cues. Those may have been characteristics of the sisters' dynamic but it was obvious once the uncle arrived that something else was going on to make people uneasy at this dinner party, something all the women at the table felt. Belinda looked at Claire and then at her uncle, who was staring at her, back at her sister and then down into her lap. Claire alternated between moving her silverware a fraction of an inch—knife to the right and back, fork to the left and back—and her eyes flashed up every few seconds to see what her uncle and his girlfriend were doing. Her uncle was looking around expectantly; his girlfriend was smoothing non-existent wrinkles from her skirt. And although Louisa had tried to chastise her brother for being late, you could see that her scolding contained something bigger than his arriving on Miami time. They were all unusually silent for a family getting together for dinner.

Claire nodded at me to serve the first course. I placed the tray of soups and toasts in the pass-through window and Rachel and Terry did their thing. Then the uncle started talking again, loud and animated, about a new project he was working on, something to do with one of the buildings downtown. He seemed to be directing his remarks only to Hal and from the way he was talking, with condescension and familiarity, whatever work the uncle did, Hal did a similar kind but the uncle was

trying to assert his expertise. It was also obvious
that no one else at the table had any knowledge of
or interest in this business that Hal and the uncle
shared but it didn't stop the uncle from talking or
most of the people at the table from behaving as
though it was the most riveting conversation they
had ever heard.

*And so I got the deal very smoothly, Hal. Ya
woulda been proud, old man. I figure it'll only take
me about six months to get the whole thing off the
ground and running. Think your guys coulda done
that?*

Professor Rick, who hadn't sat up straight nor
said a word since we'd gotten there, began to eat as
soon as his soup was set down; he was so hunched
over that his mouth was only inches from the
champagne flute after Rachel placed it in front of
him. Hal picked up his toast and took a bite while
nodding his head in the uncle's direction. Louisa's
date looked as though he didn't know what to do
so he took a sip of his wine and then a bite of his
toast and then a sip of wine and then a sip of his
soup: he was not part of this family, just Louisa's
date.

You ought to call Bernie at the city hall, Hal
told the uncle, *because he can probably help you get
the specs on that zoning.*

I don't need Bernie, the uncle said, *I have
someone to do specs.*

Who? Hal asked.

You don't know him, the uncle said.

There was a slight pause but then Hal said,

Well, Arthur King over at Bartell's has a new guy who's a computer whiz. He could hook you up.

Got it all hooked up and locked down, Hal, the uncle said.

Ok Marv, Hal said, with a bit of impatience. *Got it. Just trying to help you out a little bit.*

Why's that, Hal? Feeling guilty?

The sisters flinched.

No, not at all...couldn't be helped Marv, you know that. When Marv didn't answer, Hal said again, *I'm just trying to help you out.*

Oh, you've helped me out plenty, Marv said and looked up at his niece Belinda, who was staring at him but then immediately looked away.

That exchange sent everyone at the table to full concentration on the first course. What couldn't be helped? If Marv and Hal did the same kind of work, maybe Marv worked for Hal? Maybe Hal had to let him go? Rachel and Terry were back in the kitchen now, standing behind me setting up the salads which meant it was time for me to whisk together a vinaigrette, but I was still trying to listen, to see if I could figure out what was going on between these two men or at least to gage a reaction to my cold tomato soup, something I had not made before. The women seemed to like it, the men seemed to be drinking it just because it was there. Marv picked up his champagne flute full of soup and said *Pretty fancy—what's the big occasion?* When no one answered, he shook his head but he drank it all at once and then put the whole parmesan toast into his mouth, as if he

just wanted to get the eating part of this dinner
party over with. His girlfriend sipped and then bit,
the way it was supposed to be eaten. She seemed
comfortable with this kind of dining but not with
anything else at this dinner. She touched her hair,
shifted in her seat, patted her boyfriend Marv on
the knee.

You learn a lot from spending hours and hours
in other people's kitchens, seeing how they deal
with food and with the people they've decided to
feed. You learn that families are all entirely different
and all entirely the same. There are conflicts and
factions. There are favorites and black sheep. There
are pleasers and then there are guys like Uncle
Marv. Marv should have been named Mac or Bill
or Clint, anything but Marv, which was the name of
an old man whose time had passed and he seemed
to labor under it. His face was chiseled and just
the soft side of gaunt and when he looked at you,
you had the shameful flash of a hope that he found
you attractive. He wore faded Levis and work boots
and a worn out button-down shirt tucked in, even
though everyone else had made a clear choice to
wear their good clothes. His hair was not long but
not short and he was tan, probably from working
outside. He was aging the way women wished
they could age, with lines and creases and a little
gray hair that made him look even better than you
imagined he looked when he was young. On first
sighting, he looked like the kind of guy who could
have been discovered by a scout on a street corner,
he was that handsome and that oblivious of it; but

when you studied, there was something about his
manner—something cagey and anxious—that made
you think he was too uneasy in himself to be the
confident guy his genetics has predestined him for.
He was exciting, a little dangerous.

He sat back in his chair and then rubbed his
girlfriend's back. They looked good together—the
outdoorsy guy and the *au naturel* kind of hippie-
looking girl. She smiled tentatively at him over her
shoulder and he shook his head again. I'd done
enough parties to know he definitely did not want
to be at this one.

Maybe to break the icy quiet, or maybe for
another reason that had its roots in ancient history,
Claire suddenly said, *Belinda has some news.* She
turned to Belinda, who immediately recoiled as if
Claire had raised a weapon.

Oh yeah, what's that? Marv said, with a sneer.
*You make another million this year, Hal? You
taking your wife on another cruise?*

Not quite, Hal answered. *Not for a while,
anyway.*

We're pregnant, Belinda blurted out, *but I
thought we were saving this news for dessert.*
She said it with an urgency that sounded like an
apology.

Her mother gasped, *Oh my God. That's
thrilling, darling. I'm going to be a grandmother.*

Congratulations, the mother's date said to
Belinda. *You, too, Louisa,* he said to the mother.

That's wonderful, Marv's girlfriend said. Claire
put her arm around her sister and Hal was beaming

ear to ear but then Marv started clapping, a series
of loud slow claps with several seconds of interval
between them. Belinda looked down at her lap
and Claire looked up at me and mouthed the word
Salad.

I came out of the kitchen to help Terry remove
the first course plates and set down the salads while
Rachel refilled the waters and poured a fume blanc
Claire had chosen for the salad course. *I'll have
another one of these,* Marv said, raising his empty
scotch glass and winking at Rachel which made
her blush. Then he started laughing, which did not
make much sense except he reminded me of bad but
adorable children who did whatever they wanted
to because they knew they could. He was so much
more good-looking than the other men at the table
and although everyone always hates to admit that
looks count for anything, no one can deny that
sometimes they count for everything. Hal wasn't
bad but his hair was too short and he had bangs
that made him look like a little boy whose mother
had cut his hair with a bowl. Professor Rick,
Claire's husband, was non-descript: he was a man
with less hair and more weight than he might have
wanted but he didn't seem to care; he was the kind
of man who keeps his head down not because he's
shy but because he's not interested.

So when's little Hal due, Marv said. He was still
laughing and then he drank down the rest of his
first scotch as Rachel set down his second.

We don't know if it's a boy or a girl, Belinda
said.

Hal, Hallie, what's the difference? I'll be a great-uncle either way.

You're a great uncle, now, Belinda said in a voice so loud that it was startling. She looked sorry the moment she said it.

A great-uncle at 43, Marv said. *That deserves a toast.* He raised a forkful of Romaine and said *To the next generation of Cooper Construction. Put me right out of business this time.*

Here, here, the mother's date said but in the middle of Marv's toast so he didn't hear the last sentence and so missed the sarcasm. Marv put the forkful of salad in his mouth and then waved the empty fork in the air. Marv's girlfriend took a long sip of her wine, and everyone else looked down at their plates.

What's the matter? Marv said, *aren't we celebrating?*

Cut it out, Marvin, his sister said. She had some matriarchal clout because after she said it, everyone began to eat their salads.

I had a main course to plate, which took me away from the pass-through window. Rachel and Terry were in the kitchen stirring the sauce and taking the potatoes out of the oven. None of us could see them but I suspected we were all wondering the same thing. From the start, Marv and his girlfriend had been exiled to their own side of the table and Marv had made a point of taking those seats late. That Marv had a chip on his shoulder was obvious; everything he'd said and done since the moment he arrived supported

that. But that there was something deeper than
mere envy and angst raised my interest yet also
made it clearly none of my business. I'd catered for
anorexics, drunken hosts who'd grabbed my ass,
guests who had stolen things and when caught,
tried to blame us; once a child of ten had snuck into
my van to smoke a joint and the parents tried to
have me arrested for giving their son drugs. I was
used to being a hero and a villain, and I was very
used to being an invisible audience to all sorts of
family drama, but in the small space of this kitchen,
all the dark innuendo of the silent table made me
feel perverse. Of course we were supposed to be
there, but I felt like a voyeur.

We served sliced tenderloin with bordelaise
sauce, wedges of Potatoes Anna, asparagus roasted
with balsamic vinegar, and red cabbage sautéed
with lemon and pepper. The plates looked great: I
was very pleased with how things were going, at
least on my end. But when I looked over at Claire,
while Rachel and Terry were collecting empty salad
plates, her palpable anxiety made me feel nervous
and itchy. Before setting the plated dinners down,
Rachel poured the Bordeaux and Marv signaled
for another scotch. I felt a small knot form in my
throat. I'd done many parties where the hostess
warned us that a family member drank too much;
I'd nod my head and make sure we poured weak
drinks or smaller glasses of wine. We were practiced
at being discreet. I decided to get the drink myself
and watered it down a bit. When I set it down
by his plate, he looked up at me and said, *I'm*

celebrating—Hal's having a baby and he jabbed my
arm with his elbow as if my bringing him the third
tumbler of scotch made me complicit.

The women were oooing and aahing about the
dinner and Hal was nodding all around the table
as if he'd made the food himself. Marv said *So
that's why you got a caterer, eh? Very fancy for this
announcement. Nice touch, Claire.* I couldn't tell if
he was trying to ease the tension he'd created or if
he was mocking them for hiring us. But then Louisa
said, quite intentionally I thought, *Laura, how's
work?* and Laura, Marv's girlfriend, immediately
began a story as if she had relied on talking as a
diversion many times before.

*I have a new patient who I feel really badly for.
He's sixty-two years old and this is his first time—
his children made him see me—and he just looks
at me like I'm supposed to be the one doing all the
talking. It's frustrating,* she said, *trying to get him to
tell me what's wrong.*

*And you sure as hell aren't making enough
money for all the frustration you have and I have
listening to it,* Marv said. *You should get a new job.*

I love my job, Laura said but Marv ignored her.

Maybe you can be a nanny to Baby Hal? and
he wiped up the bordelaise on his plate with a roll,
almost as if he was purposely trying to rebel against
what he perceived as the formality of this dinner.
Keep it in the family, he said with his mouth full.
He was the only man I had ever seen who could
treat his own family so terribly while talking with
his mouth full and still manage to be appealing.

Maybe it's time you made your own family?
Louisa said. She was reaching a limit with her
brother.

Finally kicking me out of yours? Marv said.
*Hey, don't bother. Remember, I don't live in your
attic anymore.*

*I'm just saying maybe you and Laura ought to
think about getting married,* Louisa said.

Laura smiled at Louisa's statement and then
rolled her eyes but in a kind way. Marv slapped
her on the back a little too hard and said *Sure,
I'll marry old Laura here...when I make a million
dollars.*

You mean when pigs fly, Claire said but as soon
as she said it, her eyes closed and her fists clenched,
as if she was trying to catch the words and take
them back.

What the hell's that supposed to mean? Marv
said, the fast anger making his face a dark red.
Marv had barely been able to stop looking at
Belinda all night but it was also clear that he could
hardly stand to look at Claire and you could tell
he was vindicated, even happy, that Claire had
provided the ultimate insult. *You don't think I can
make a million dollars, like Big Hal here?*

You'll make a million dollars, Uncle Marv,
Belinda offered, but it was in a weak and shaky
voice. He flashed her a big smile and Claire gave
her a dirty look but none of it mattered: Marv and
Claire were in battle. Rachel, Terry and I were in
the kitchen, waiting to collect the dinner plates but
now that didn't seem like it was going to happen

any time soon.

What's the matter, Claire? You think I'm going to be a big loser because I don't work for my pal Hal here anymore?

Hal shook his head very slightly and picked up his glass of wine. So my speculations had been right: Marv had worked for Hal. It was obvious that Hal had been through this before and either knew better than to get involved or no longer wanted to.

That's not what I meant, Claire said. *I think you can make a hundred million if you want. I just meant that you and Laura have been together for ten years and...*

Then I made a decision to go out and clear the plates: I nodded to Rachel and Terry and we all went. I wanted to save Claire, who was just trying to have a dinner party in honor of her sister's good news, and Belinda, whose wide eyes and barely eaten dinner seemed to imply that she knew her good news, among other things, had contributed to all the trouble. And I wanted to stop Marv, the only person causing and enjoying all the discomfort.

Experience told me that our presence in the dining room would at least defer an impending explosion since clients tended to care more about not embarrassing themselves in front of the help than they did about fighting. But this family was beyond any experience I had had.

Ten years but who's counting, Marv continued as if we weren't even there, as if I wasn't leaning down in front of him to lift up his empty plate. *We're still trying to figure it out.*

Figure what out? Louisa said but then Laura
attempted a rescue.

We're not the marrying kind, she said with a
laugh. No one laughed back.

You know us, she went on, *besides, I don't want
to marry your uncle until he's a millionaire: I'm sick
of working. I want to lay around watching tv and
eating bon-bons.*

That might have done it except for Hal's
next observation, which was either innocent or
intentional—I had no idea. *Right,* he said. *You're
the most industrious person I know. When was the
last time you watched a whole television show?* and
Laura, so obviously trying to please everyone said,
*well, there's always so much to do around the house
and the yard. Marv works so hard, I can't just lay
around...*

So it's my fault now? Marv said.

No, honey, Laura said, and she put her hand on
his back. He shifted away under her touch. *Come
on,* she said, *you know I'm kidding. I don't know
how to lay around. That's why we get along so well,
we're the same.*

But anyone could tell that wasn't true.

Claire was a taut wire, Belinda looked sick.
Their mother was tapping her fingers on her wine
glass as if she wanted more but it was half full and
I felt as though Rachel and Terry and I couldn't
get the plates off the table and into the kitchen fast
enough. If we broke this fancy china, I'd be happy
to pay for it. Then Laura must have decided to see if
she could just start over.

Hey, great meal, she said to me and then, *I hope you have some cards with you.*

For what? Marv asked. *You think we're going to have a catered dinner anytime soon?*

Laura tried to deflect his anger, to turn it in another direction that might snuff it out. *Who knows?* she said. *Your birthday's coming up.*

So is yours, he said, his voice registering slightly less of the edge it had had the moment before, making me understand him a bit more—I knew people, mostly men, who could control a table or a room or a life with their anger by giving it and then taking it away without warning. *And hey,* he continued, *maybe you're right: we're going to be 44, too old to make our own food. Great Aunt Laura and Great Uncle Marv—codgers who want to throw a party but can't get off the couch. Get the card.* Then he turned to me and said, *Don't bother bringing bonbons. Laura here is too industrious to eat them.*

Hal stood up. I thought he was going to put a stop to all this when he said, *Well, I've been waiting all night to do this,* and he excused himself and headed into the hallway by the front door; he opened the hall closet and bent down to get something. Rachel walked around the table asking if anyone wanted coffee with their dessert but no one did; everyone except Belinda wanted more wine. Marv wanted another scotch. Rachel went to get the drinks while Terry filled the waters and the pitcher again. Despite the tension, we still prided ourselves in our service.

But I wanted to get out of there more than I had at any party I could remember. I began cutting and plating the chocolate-raspberry tart when Hal came back into the dining room with a big paper bag. Claire signaled me to wait on dessert.

We don't know if it's a boy or a girl so I got some stuff for either one. First he pulled out a small round glass bowl and then a plastic bag full of water; a goldfish was swimming around in it. *The first of our pets,* he said, dumping the goldfish into the bowl

How cute, his mother-in-law said. *What's its name?*

Haven't named it yet, Hal said, *but we will* and he winked at his wife. Belinda's shoulders sunk a bit, the tension that had kept them raised and still since her uncle had arrived finally giving way, and a grateful smile appeared on her face. She looked down at the big bag at Hal's feet and then up at Hal's face, as if she knew her husband would be able to turn this into a celebration after all. He was boyish and upbeat and I liked him but I could see how he would get on Marv's last nerve. He had the real confidence of the naturally rich, the easily pleased.

OK, next, Hal said, fishing through the bag. He started to pull something out and then said, *No not yet...I'll save these for last.* He was grinning. Marv yawned. Then Hal pulled out a stuffed bear: it was a panda, black and white and fluffy. I heard Rachel behind me say she thought that the bear was cute, and I motioned for her to be quiet. Although I still wasn't sure how to gage what was happening here, one thing I knew for certain was that we did not belong to this party.

Too adorable, Laura said and Marv's head shot up and turned on her, as if she had just screamed out an obscenity. *What?* she whispered and he just glared at her. Everyone saw it—they were all at a small dining room table—and everyone looked as surprised as I felt: Laura had done nothing but said that a stuffed animal was cute. But no one was about to contradict Uncle Marv.

Except Claire. She had had a lot of wine and apparently enough of this. *It is too adorable,* she said, *for a boy or girl. Rick's boys are in high school but they still have their stuffed animals.*

Marv snorted.

What? Claire said. *What's wrong with that? They're big guys, they play football and baseball but when we fixed up the basement for them when they stay with us, they each brought a couple of teddy bears from when they were little. It's cute. It means something.*

That's how we learned that Professor Rick had been married before and had two kids. It explained his lack of interest in the drama at this dinner table. He had probably had enough drama of his own.

Everything means something, Marv said, *just ask Dr. Laura here. Isn't that right, dear?*

Louisa's date looked up but everyone else at the table just looked down or straight ahead, blank-faced. Then Louisa turned to her date and explained, *Laura's a psychologist.*

Yeah, I got that from the story she was telling before, he said but he still looked confused.

That's why she's Dr. Laura, Louisa said, as if that would clear everything up for him. *She's got a Ph.D.*

But they don't pay her for it, Marv said standing up. *I'm getting another drink,* he said.

Wait, Hal said, as if he knew that another scotch might escalate what already seemed like a race to a finish line, *you might like this next thing. I was saving it for last but I think it will be fun. And we'll need to be good at this by the time the kid grows up, to defend ourselves.*

Marv sat back down but signaled Terry to get him a drink by holding up his empty glass. Hal was rummaging around in his big paper bag and everyone except Marv was looking over eagerly. But when Terry returned with the scotch, Laura tensed up and Claire squinted but it was too late: he took it out of her hand before it reached the table and took a dramatic sip. *Thank God,* he said, just as Hal was saying,

Ok, what do you think of these?

He pulled a plastic bag out of the paper bag and inside were squirt guns. Little plastic ones in bright green and orange and yellow.

Oh you're a genius, Hal, Marv said.

Guns, that's great, his mother-in-law said, and her brother let out a big sigh as if now, finally, someone at this table agreed with him that Hal was a jerk

Oh, Mom, Belinda said. *They're squirt guns.*

All kids have squirt guns. Claire and I had them when we were little. While she was talking, Hal was passing the squirt guns around the table; he had one for each dinner guest and people started filling them with water from the pitchers on the table. Laura filled hers and Marv's.

Not me, Marv said, *isn't that right Sis? I didn't have squirt guns when I was growing up. Of course, you're a lot older than me so maybe you had one when you were little...you had a lot of things by the time I finally came along.*

Marv was obviously twenty-some years younger than his sister but the story behind that didn't seem as though it would be coming to me and Rachel and Terry anytime soon.

I got you a squirt gun when I got them for the girls, Marvin, Louisa said. *You never wanted for anything when you lived in my house.*

Marv burst out laughing. *No, how could I have wanted for anything, living in your attic, upstairs from you and Frank and my nieces. I had everything a guy could need.*

Marvin, please, his sister said, *let's not do this, ok? Why do you always have to do this?*

It wasn't hard to figure out what he was doing, or that he did it every time the family got together. Now I understood the seating arrangement.

Uncle Marv, please, Claire said but he ignored her. Like a shadow, Terry slid in between guests and refilled the water pitchers. But even if she had made herself solid and known, if she had leaned into him or accidentally dripped some water into his lap,

Marv would not have noticed her. He had his hands palm-flat on the table, was sitting up as straight as solider, and the only thing it looked like he could see was the enemy in front of him.

Hey, you're right, I had a squirt gun, too. But wasn't I in my twenties then, Lou? The girls were what? Ten, eleven? But you got us all squirt guns. Thanks. I didn't feel left out.

Feeling left out, at that moment, would have been a blessing I would have received with great relief. Although no one at the table paid us the least bit of attention, it was impossible not to know we were there, and even more impossible for us to pretend that we weren't the unwilling observers of a family feud that was escalating at an alarming rate. I looked at Laura, to see if maybe she had a plan. But it was Belinda who made the attempt.

You still managed to squirt us every chance you got, she said, and she picked up her squirt gun as if she wanted to shoot her uncle, maybe for old time's sake, maybe for now. But it made a difference: when she spoke to him, Marv turned to her and he looked at her so intently, it seemed as if the past had returned to soften him. He looked almost sorry, but then answered in a way that revealed where his real sorrow lay.

Only you, Linnie. You were a little fireball then. I had to squirt you whenever I could, Marv said. Claire stiffened, Louisa looked away and I clenched my own fists against my temples. I did not want to think about what he might be saying. I did not want to look at Rachel and Terry to see if they were fearing the same thing. I had no idea what could happen next but then Belinda, the only person at the table who had not had any alcohol, must have thought if she took the joke wider, higher, she could make it fly away.

I never could run fast enough, then, Belinda said and it seemed as though she was going to squirt her uncle right between the eyes but when he put his hands up in mock defense, she turned the gun on Hal and fired a long squirt of water into her husband's shoulder. Marv's eyes narrowed into blades and he flicked his squirt gun across the table. It stopped when it hit the water pitcher. At the sound, Belinda turned back to him quickly. He was staring right through her. She put her head down and then without looking, feebly squirted her mother.

Stop it, Louisa said, trying to sound playful. *Just because you're pregnant doesn't mean I won't squirt you back.* She squirted Belinda and then waited. When her youngest daughter didn't react, she squirted Claire, *So you don't feel left out, dear,* she said.

Always so thoughtful, aren't you Lou? Always mothering. You could learn something from your mother, Linnie, Marv said, but it was clear he didn't mean it. Belinda, who no one else at the table had called Linnie, looked at her sister.

Cute, Mom, Claire said and it almost sounded like relief. *Remember these, honey?* she said to her husband and squirted him in the ear. Professor Rick cracked a smile, the first one of the evening. *I'll get you back,* he said to his wife, *when you least expect it.* The mother's date picked up his squirt gun and aimed it at Hal: *seems like you ought to have a squirt,* he said, and fired a stream of water at Hal's chest. *En guard,* Hal said, and fired one back at the date.

Maybe Hal was a genius after all. If it was easy for this family to pass through what had just happened, then it would be simple for Rachel, Terry and me to get through the rest of the night. We could hold the dessert while the dinner guests squirted each other and while I watched I realized that, in fact, we'd seen weirder things. At one dinner party, an elderly aunt got so drunk on sherry that she had climbed into a fourteen year old boy's lap. We'd done a small second wedding once where the bride had stuck the cake knife into her groom's arm because the photographer had mistaken her for another woman in a white suit, one he had seen in the hallway with the groom moments before. This party, although tense and odd, was turning out to be fine, for everyone except Uncle Marv but in my view, it was seven to one so what could he do? It was obvious that no one was going to include him, to squirt him, but he didn't seem to care: he was half way through his fifth scotch and as soon as his niece Belinda had turned her attention back to her husband Hal, Marv's face had transformed into a scowl that said he didn't want to have anything to do with this anyway.

Laura was fingering her squirt gun, turning it over in her hands as if she was examining it for prints. Everyone else at the table was looking slyly at each other and periodically someone would fire off a stream of water at someone who was looking slyly at someone else. Hal was at the head of the table and everyone to his left was laughing and firing the squirt guns. On the other side of the table, Marv and Laura just sat watching.

Even Professor Rick seemed to be enjoying himself; on either side of him, his wife and her sister blasted him and he just let the water run down his face while he decided on whom to retaliate first. The mother's date was holding his gun in a police stance and moving it side to side, to protect himself and to surprise an unwitting target. Rachel and Terry and I watched them and shrugged our shoulders: we got paid by the hour.

At one point, I thought maybe Marv had surrendered and given in to his family's levity. He had leaned back and had one hand on his drink and his other on the back of Laura's chair but when I looked more closely, I could see that what I had first interpreted as resignation was really rigid contempt; he was stiff as a board and seemed to tighten even more as it became more and more obvious that everyone else was having a great time and ignoring him. Even Laura joined in, laughing at all the jokes and squirting Belinda back when a stream of water blasted into her chest.

But then Laura turned to look at Marv. Maybe she began to feel bad that she was playing and Marv was being excluded from the game. After all, this was his family. Maybe the wine had eased her

apprehensions, maybe it had made her delusional.
Whatever it was, she looked at her boyfriend in a
way that said—at least to me—that she thought
she could make all things here right. And even
though these people were more unpredictable than
any clients I had ever had, I knew instinctively that
whatever it was she had decided was dead wrong.

She reached over to pick up Marv's squirt gun
and give it to him but he scowled and shook his
head in disdain. Then she pointed hers at him and
he said in voice so loud that it overrode all the
laughter, *don't even think about it.*

I wanted to say it, too. I wanted to say don't
even think about it and although I would never
have given into that impulse, it wouldn't have
mattered if I did. It was obvious that Laura had no
intentions of thinking about it. There was no way
she was going to squirt her boyfriend. But then
Belinda did.

It was a tiny squirt of water and it hit Marv
on the side of his forehead and trickled down his
cheek. It was the very smallest of things but a pall
came over the table, so black and final, you would
have thought someone had been murdered. I heard
Belinda whimper and felt my own pulse snap.

It would have seemed completely rude, not
to mention unprofessional, to see me and Rachel
and Terry standing at the pass-through window
watching this but we did not move because we
did not exist. Marv took his hand off the back of
Laura's chair and used it to wipe the water off his
face. Laura looked at him with an uneasy smile, the

unused squirt gun still in her hand.

He was looking at her, too, but with the expression of a weary parent who was tired of saying the same thing over and over again to a child who needed to learn a lesson once and for all. He looked away and took a long swallow of his drink. No one moved. When he set the drink down, he scanned the surface of the table as if he was looking for his own plastic weapon. But he was not; no mere squirt gun was going to accomplish what he had in mind. In one smooth but very deliberate movement, he lifted the water pitcher that Terry had just refilled and poured its entire contents very slowly over Laura's head.

The force of the moment sent Rachel and Terry so close to me that their arms were pressed against my sides. I took their hands. The table looked like a dinner party from a wax museum. There was so much water in that pitcher that Laura's long curly black hair was drenched completely straight, dripping into her lap, down her back, onto the table and the floor.

How's that for a squirt? Marv said, in a tone of voice that said he believed he had done the right thing, the only thing.

Laura lifted one hand and moved a long strand of sopping hair out of her eye. It didn't seem as though anyone else at the table was going to be able to break the horrible spell and I thought I should do something except I didn't know what that should be. Over a long career, I'd preempted many crises and stopped some once they'd started. I'd carefully

taken a raised carving knife out of the hand of
an irate father-in-law who hated his daughter's
husband and looked like he might stab him when
the son-in-law declared in front of the Christmas
ham that he didn't eat meat. At a small dinner of
four, I had been clearing plates when the hostess
stood up and admitting she'd had too much wine,
fell backward into my arms that just happened to
be there. But here at this party, I had no idea what
to do.

But then, very quietly, Laura pushed her chair
back, stood up, delicately gathered up her gauzy
skirt so the water in her lap wouldn't fall onto the
floor, and headed toward the guest bathroom down
the hall. Belinda and Claire stood up at the same
time and followed her. Marv turned back to his
drink.

Come on, I whispered to Rachel and Terry.
Grab some towels. We went out to the table and
while Rachel wiped Laura's chair and the floor
around it and Terry cleared the glasses and pitcher
away from Laura's empty place, I sopped up the
water that had collected on the table. No one said a
word, not to each other, not to us. We had to move
in and out between everyone, excuse ourselves to
lean over them and crawl around their knees to
sop up water that was moving toward their chairs.
Although water was getting absorbed up by towels,
glasses were being moved and pitchers were being
taken away, we were entirely invisible and no one
seemed at all astounded by the magical way the
crisis was being tidied up.

The sounds I could hear were voices coming from the bathroom but I couldn't make out who was talking or what was being said. Then the bathroom door opened and I stood up straight. But the three women did not return to the table; seconds later, we all heard the bedroom door click closed.

Marv finished his drink with one hand and rubbed his neck with the other. Finally someone spoke. It was Louisa.

Why on earth did you do that? she said.

Stay out of it, Lou.

Stay out of it? she said. *You forced us all into it.*

Drop it, Lou. I mean it. I didn't want to be squirted with a stupid fucking squirt gun. Laura knows better. She knew what would happen.

Huh? Laura didn't squirt you. Belinda did. This time the person speaking was Louisa's date.

You stay out of it, too, pal, Marv said. It seemed as though he did not remember his sister's date's name. *But for what it's worth, Laura knew what would happen. She knows me.*

Her loss, Professor Rick said and he stood up. He had been so hunched over during the dinner that I was surprised to see how tall he was. *Get up,* he said to Marv but Marv didn't move. *Get up and get out of my house, Marvin.*

This isn't your house, Rick, Marv said with a smirk, *it's Claire's. Your house is about a mile away, with an ex-wife and two kids in it. Lucky you, this house came with my niece, her mother's money, and an extra room for your kids and their teddy bears.*

What is it with all you people? What is it you don't get?

Just then Laura and Belinda and Claire came out of the bedroom. Belinda had been crying, her eye make-up still darkening the space under her eyes though you could tell she'd tried to wipe it off. Claire's fury was plastered onto her lip-sticked mouth. Someone had put Laura's wet hair in two braids and she looked like a child, innocent and relieved: whatever she had been anxious about earlier had obviously materialized and she seemed calmer, now that it was over. She sat down in her chair and put her wrists on the table but when Marv placed his hand on her hand, she moved her arms into her lap.

We were back in the kitchen. I was standing at the pass-through window and Terry and Rachel were trying their best to finish up the rest of the dishes as quietly but as quickly as possible so we could make a fast departure as soon as the right moment arose. I had considered moving to the back of the kitchen where they couldn't see me but there was still the dessert to serve and even though it didn't seem like anyone would be wanting it, I thought maybe Claire might request it, to create a diversion.

But she took her seat back at the table and never looked at me so I backed away from the window. On instinct, I fit the pieces of the tart back into the pan, covered it with plastic wrap and put it in the refrigerator. Then I whispered to Rachel and Terry that even though there were still some

glasses on the table, very quietly we should pack up
our things and go. At the table, everyone sat there
silently. People who had drinks were drinking them;
others were staring blankly into the space in front
of their eyes. At any other party, the troublemaker
would be escorted out or at the very least asked to
leave. But families were different.

Except for the sounds we couldn't help
but make as we loaded our gear into bags and
boxes, there was no noise in that house. Every
once in a while, I'd look over my shoulder to see
everyone still in their seats at the table but no one
was speaking. Marv had not stood when Rick
commanded he leave and now Rick had taken his
seat again as well. Claire had her hand in his in his
lap. There was a bizarre stillness, like a tableau,
frozen back to the slow-motion moment when
Marv had poured the pitcher of water over Laura's
head. It seemed as though the dinner party had
stopped right there and decided not to regress or
proceed.

A few minutes later, we were done and it was
time for us to go. I knew it was best if we just
slipped out silently but just then, the doorbell rang.

That would be my cab, Laura said, and she
stood.

Don't be an ass, Laura, Marv said.

Ignoring him, Laura once again became the
person she had been when she arrived. She told the
whole table she was sorry. Then she thanked Claire
and Rick for dinner, congratulated Belinda and Hal
on the baby, said it was good to see Louisa and nice

to meet her date, and turned toward the kitchen. I heard her call my name and I went to the pass-through window.

Wonderful meal, she said to me.

I was spellbound but managed to say, *thank you.*

Superb food. And service. Really. This couldn't have been easy for you guys. Thanks.

Jesus, Marv said.

Thank you, I said to Laura. And then seeing her stand there for a minute as if she didn't know what she was supposed to do next, I said, *I'll get the door.*

Marv followed Laura outside but backed off when the cab driver got out to open the door for her. She got in the back and the cabbie got in the front and drove Laura away. When Marv came back toward the house, I was still standing at the door.

She worked for a caterer for a long time, he said to me, *while she was in college and then in graduate school. I'll take a couple of your cards for her but Laura's a great cook.*

He went to the bar to fix himself another drink. Rachel and Terry had cleared the rest of the glasses and dishes from table and were starting to wash them. Someone had taken all the squirt guns and put them back into the big paper bag. You could see the brown paper turning dark from water leaking from the nozzles. I had decided that Rachel, Terry and I would leave, that I would call Claire the next day to see about getting paid, but on my way back into the kitchen, Claire called out my name and said now would be a good time to serve the dessert.

The Tavern

Monday nights are "Sunday Night Dinner" at The Tavern because Sunday nights are "Breakfast for Dinner" and even though Wade knows people love having a good excuse to eat bacon and eggs and hash browns and sausage and cinnamon rolls for supper, he thinks that maybe by Monday, they'll feel like they missed something. I had been at the spot on the turnpike when I realized I was hungry, that I'd been hungry for some time.

For these last two weeks, since the accident, Kip has been managing the whole place for Wade, which is nice and all but just reminds everyone at The Tavern more of the awful thing, that Roberta is gone, that there was another man in the car, that Wade is somewhere without his wife, sad and grieving.

It's "all you can eat" every night if you order the special dinner and I am just finishing my second helping of roast beef when I see Wade coming out of the kitchen. He goes behind the bar and pours himself a Coke and drinks it down fast. Kip's behind the bar but he's waiting on two people I've never seen in The Tavern before and besides Wade is the kind of guy who does things for himself, even if there's someone there to do it for him. He puts

the glass in the bar sink and heads back toward
the kitchen. I want to say hello to him but he never
looks my way.

I want to say some other things, too, like truly
I am sorry for him about Roberta and that I'm
also sorry we can't no longer say what we were
saying when we first found out, that he shouldn't
worry about who that other man was in the car
because it could have been anyone, like maybe a
cousin he'd never heard of or maybe just some guy
she was giving a ride home. Because Roberta was
headed in the opposite direction of where she and
Wade lived so maybe she was just doing someone
a favor—though she wasn't the type—driving him
home, when her car went off the turnpike and then
into the canal. But we can't say that now.

Wade is in the kitchen but now that I know he's
back to work, I take another roll out of the basket
and use it to mop up the gravy on my plate. I'm not
full but I was done. I know when enough is enough.
And at home I have some chocolate ice cream that
I want to eat later during the 9:00 **Law & Order**
on the TV. But I pull the roll across the plate slow
and eat it in little bites so it'll take longer and also
so that maybe Wade will come back out and I can
catch his eye and have him come over here, so I can
say I am sorry and also, maybe, tell him the things
that I have been seeing and thinking.

When I was at the spot on the turnpike where
Roberta had drove out of the world, I got my
cane and got out of my car and went over to the
guard rail. Someone had put a wooden cross in the

ground there and all around it there were some new
flowers. Planted ones, and I wonder if Wade knows
who did that or even if he did it himself. The water
was flat with just a little ripple and it's hard to
imagine why, before the car started to sink, Roberta
and that man couldn't have just opened the doors
and got out. There's a lot of stuff on the news all
the time about what to do when your car goes in
a canal because cars go in canals in South Florida
all the time. They tell you not to panic. If the car
is already sinking, you're supposed to wait for it
to be completely under the water and then lower
your windows. No one says this is going to be easy
and, sure, when you open the window the car will
fill with water but then the pressure gets balanced
and you just swim out. If you have the kind of car
that has electric windows, you're supposed to keep
one of these tools in your car that has a sharp little
point on it so you can break your window and
swim out to safety. When you think about it this
way, it seems like there would be a lot of time to
figure out how to get out. That would be good for
me because I have an old car, the kind where you
have to roll the windows down and with that and
my bad leg, I'd need the extra time if I ever drove
into a canal. In the news it said that Roberta and
the man were still holding hands when they found
them.

　　Crystal comes and takes my plate and brings
me a cup of coffee. The coffee cups are that thick
white kind, too wide at the brim so by the time you
get the coffee and put some cream in it, it isn't even

close to hot anymore but that's all right because even though I always have coffee after I eat, I never drink much of it. It's just something to do. I take a sip and then I see some plaid out of the corner of my eye and Wade is walking across the restaurant toward the cash register so I read over my bill and reach across the table to get my purse so I can go and pay.

Wade could be a TV star if anyone would come to Miami Shores and see him in his jeans and work shirts and ball caps. He's big and fit and has a long thin good nose and dark brown eyes and he doesn't smile that much but when he does, it just about knocks you over. Maybe he shaves every other day or every three days but he always has some beard on his face which just makes him look like he's too busy thinking about things to think about what he looks like. That's what it's like a lot of times with people who are born gorgeous. Well, not all people. Roberta was a beauty queen. A real one. And you just know she thought about the beauty stuff all the time. She was from a small town in Ohio and had been the Circleville Pumpkin Queen when she was in high school but since I knew her, she really worked at keeping those looks. She had her hair colored and done up and her nails painted at all times and she wore really tight skirts and shirts that showed her cleavage and she still had her figure so she looked pretty good.

I watch Wade go over to the cash register and start to count the money. He looks like he's lost some weight but who can blame him? Grief takes your appetite. His jeans look more baggy than usual and his shirt is out and unbuttoned so I can see how his undershirt is coming out from his pants, even though he has a belt. I am staring at him so that maybe he'll look up and I can wave and he'll see that I'm getting ready to come over and pay and say hello but he is concentrating on counting so I get my money out and think I'll just go pay and then I can say something. Maybe something that will help.

"Good roast beef tonight, Wade," I say.

"Thanks, Belle." He says this to me without looking up.

"You doing ok?" I ask.

"Sure," he says. "You got your bill?"

"Sure," I say, and hand it over. I have the exact amount in my hand but I throw it back into the bottom of my purse and pull out a twenty dollar bill instead, so Wade will have to take some time to make me some change.

"Nothing smaller?" he says. My bill is only $6.95. The all-you-can-eat "Sunday Dinner" roast beef at The Tavern is a deal.

"No siree," I say.

"All right then," he says, and starts to make my change. I'm thinking about what would be a good thing to say to Wade. I want to tell him about the wooden cross and the new flowers but then he is putting the change in my hand and closing the drawer and saying "Thanks, Belle" and walking away all at the same time.

In the two weeks since Roberta and that man in her car died, there has been lots of stuff on the

TV and in the newspaper about what might have
happened to them but no one seems to know for
sure. At first they wouldn't release the man's name
but then they did and it was Sam. Sam Billings.
There's a wife in Opa-locka and a couple of kids
and the wife said in an interview that she didn't
know Roberta, had never heard of her, and didn't
know why Sam was in the car or that he ever even
went to Miami Shores. Maybe it was the way
the reporter wrote it that made it seem that Mrs.
Billings didn't really care, either. She said she didn't
know how Sam would ever meet Roberta—in the
paper she called her *this Roberta*—and I knew
what she meant because the Shores isn't the kind
of place you just happened into. Miami is big and
real spread out and there are lots of places people
always go to when they come here like South Beach
and Aventura and South Miami and Coconut Grove
but the Shores is a little community and mostly it's
just those of us who live here who are here. Maybe
if Sam Billings had stayed in Opa-Locka, none of
this would have happened.

Roberta didn't have to work so she didn't and
even though sometimes she hung out at The Tavern,
she never did any work when she was there, even
when it was real busy and Wade could've used
some help. She thought she was a customer, even
though I don't think I ever once saw her pay. She'd
sit on a stool at the bar and have a Bloody Mary
or a Whiskey Sour and talk to Kip or to one of her
girlfriends who she sometimes brought in with her.
I remember one time, and this was some years back,

when there was something on the TV about how
you could tie the stem from a maraschino cherry
into a knot with your tongue and Roberta and one
of her girlfriends sat there eating cherry after cherry
trying to do it. Their tongues were curling and
flapping and they were making their lips puff out
like kissing and people were laughing and clapping
and cheering them on. The Tavern's not that big
and Roberta and her friend were pretty loud so
everyone there knew what they were doing and it
was like a show.

   I don't know what she did when she wasn't at
The Tavern except that Wade always was there so
Roberta could have been doing anything. Maybe
she met Sam Billings on one of those nights when
she wasn't at the bar. After they reported Sam's
name and interviewed his wife, they interviewed
Wade but he just kept saying "no comment" over
and over again, no matter what they asked. Even
when that reporter from Channel 6, the one who
has her hair different almost every day, asked
him if he and Roberta had any kids, he said "No
comment."

   Tuesday night is Pasta Night at The Tavern and
they have it set up on a buffet. It's the same every
week—lasagna, manicotti, a pan of meatballs, a
pan of sausage with peppers, different kinds of
spaghetti, a tomato sauce and a white sauce, and
a big bowl of salad with olives in it and also those
little green peppers that aren't that hot. First I have
the salad and then I have everything else but one at
a time so I never have to try and fit too many things

on my plate. The meatballs are good so sometimes after I've had everything else, I go back for a few more meatballs.

"Get enough to eat Belle," Crystal asks when she brings me my cold coffee.

"You bet," I say, "always do."

The whole time I'm here, and it's a long time because it takes a long time to eat some of everything on Pasta Night, Wade is sitting at the bar having a coke. There's a bowl in front of him that probably has some spaghetti in it but he isn't eating. He's tall so his feet are on the floor and he's tapping one of them. Tapping it the whole time I'm here watching him. I'm watching him while I eat so that if he looks over at me I can wave him over to my table, see if he wants some company to eat with. In case that happens, I'm careful not to spill sauce on my blouse since I'm looking at Wade and not at my fork or my food. But he doesn't turn around. When Kip isn't busy, he stands in front of Wade and they talk about something. Maybe they're talking about what happened, trying to figure it out.

Roberta and Wade's house is on NE 104th Street in a nice part of the Shores that has lots of trees and kids. I like kids so I drive down that street all the time when I run my errands and people are always outside, having a beer and watching their kids run around the front yards. One of the neighbors either bought or made this big cardboard policeman and put it right in the middle of NE 104th Street so when you're driving you have to slow down because there are so many little kids

there. Roberta and Wade's house is in the middle
of the street; it is painted a light brown color and
someone takes good care of their yard because the
grass is always cut and neat and they have some
flowering bushes on either side of the front door.
Whoever is doing the yard is still doing it, even after
Roberta drove into the canal, because I was just
driving by there today and it still looks very nice.

Almost every night, one of the networks on my
cable shows reruns of **Law & Order**. They start at
7:00 and on most nights go until 11:00. I watch
them all. In the middle of the 9:00 one, I get some
ice cream, or maybe a Popsicle if it's really hot
and I don't feel like doing the work of scooping
the ice cream out. I love all the people on Law &
Order so even though I've seen them all, I watch
them again. My favorite cop is Detective Goran,
from *Criminal Intent*. He knows everything. He
has a third eye, sees things no one else can see and
things only someone who is very brilliant would
know. A third eye and a second sense, he has these
special things and so he solves all the crimes. His
partner is Detective Eames and I like her, too—she's
good—but you can tell that she knows he's the
one who knows everything and even though she
always looks really proud of him when he figures
something out, you can tell she expects him to
figure everything out anyway. If I could, I'd call
him and tell him about Roberta and Sam Billings.
I'd take him to the place where they drove into the
canal holding hands and I bet he'd see something
there—something on the ground or in the water or

maybe in the air or the trees—and be able to tell
Wade what happened. Goran never misses anything.

Ever since Roberta died, I've been watching
the **Law & Order** reruns more carefully because I
think maybe I'll learn a trick or two from Goran
and Eames and might be able to use it to figure
something out. You never know. I watch the **Law
& Orders** and then the next day, I go back to that
spot on the turnpike where the guardrail is still
busted through and I look around. I take a Baggie
and some tweezers just in case I find something that
could be a clue.

At just about the same time everyday, I realize
that I'm hungry and head over to The Tavern,
already knowing what I'm going to eat because
every night is some special night and on the nights
when I don't like the special, I order off the menu.
Wednesday is Chinese Night and I'm not wild
about egg rolls and chop suey so tonight I'm having
the fried chicken. It comes with three sides and I
order applesauce, cole slaw and corn. Things you
order off the menu are not "all-you-can-eat" but
if I'm not satisfied after my first plate, Crystal or
Clara—the other waitress who has my section when
Crystal is off—bring me another plate and don't
charge me for it.

I always eat slow which is good for the
digestion but since Wade's come back to work,
I've been thinking more and more about Roberta
and want to ask him some questions so I take even
more time. I haven't seen any clues at the scene but
Roberta and Sam Billings holding hands is in my

mind all the time and I want to talk to someone
about it. I wish I knew Goran because he could
probably figure out what everything means. I'm
thinking maybe Roberta and Sam grabbed each
other's hands when the car went in because they
were so scared and didn't know what else to do.
Maybe they were too scared to do what you're
supposed to do—wait, roll the window down, swim
out of the car—and so just grabbed onto each other.
Or maybe they had already been holding hands and
maybe then it happened faster than I think it would
and they just went down like that. If they were
already holding hands, maybe they were looking
into each other's eyes too and so didn't even see
the car going off the turnpike and into the water.
Maybe they were smiling and didn't know. If that
was the case, I'd say they were pretty lucky.

And I know something about luck. At the
Publix grocery store, where I used to work stocking
shelves and moving things around and trying to
keep the store looking nice, I got really lucky. I
worked there for about fifteen years, ever since I
finished high school. But seven years ago, I was
on the ladder putting wine glasses and champagne
glasses on the shelf that's at the very top of all the
shelves of wine. We were selling them for $1.99
each, even though they were real glass and not the
plastic kind we sold in the picnic aisle that come
four to a box. These glasses weren't in boxes, they
were all just laying in a grocery cart, so I had to
pick two up at a time, climb up the ladder, put them
on the shelf, go back down the ladder to get two

more and so on. It took a long time and made me tired and what I didn't know was that I was using one of the Publix old ladders instead of one of the new ones and I was at the top pushing a champagne glass way far over to the right when the step gave way and then I was falling and fell hard right into the cart with all the glasses, with my one leg half in and half out of the cart and the other one caught by the ankle around where the cart handle is attached. Some of those glasses broke when I fell and I got some glass in my eyelids and my face and my neck and I remember hearing all the people asking me if I was all right but I don't remember what I said. But I do know I heard someone say, "she sure is lucky."

They called an ambulance and my husband but the ambulance got there first. I thought I was all right even though my face hurt and I could tell I was bleeding but I could still see and hear and figured once they let me get up, I could probably walk, too. But that wasn't exactly true since there was a problem with my ankle and after they stitched me up, I knew it when I tried to get up out of the hospital bed and go into the hall to look for my husband. The nurses were mad and made me stay in the bed and when I asked them where my husband was, they said no one could find him.

He showed up, though it wasn't until the next morning. By then, all the skin around my stitches had swelled and gone purple and when my husband saw me, he actually screamed.

My social security and disability checks come on Friday so on Thursday nights when I go to

The Tavern, I don't have as much money as I do
at the beginning of the week and on the weekend,
but it works out pretty well because Wade made
Thursday nights "Ladies Night" which means all
appetizers are half off for ladies and there's so much
going on there on Thursdays that I can just eat two
appetizers for the price of one really slowly and
watch.

It seems like all the girls in the Shores, young
and old, come to The Tavern on Ladies Night; they
come because all the men come, too. The men come
for them and they know it. Sometimes I see some
of the girls I used to work with at Publix and they
wave and ask how I'm doing. I'm doing fine, I say.
They get all dolled up to come here and then they
sit at the bar and sip drinks and wait for the men
who will come up and talk to them and buy them
some more drinks. Some of these girls I know have
boyfriends and two I know have husbands but that
doesn't seem to make a difference on Ladies Night.

Wade's wearing another plaid shirt but he's got
it tucked in because he's staying out here the whole
time tonight. This is where the action is and I stay
longer too because on Thursday nights, the cable
network shows sports instead of **Law & Order**. I'm
looking around the way Goran would if he was
here because if I've learned anything from him, it's
that you can see the same thing or the same person
every single day and then one day, if you're looking
really carefully, you see it different. You see it for
what it really is.

Goran almost always wears the same old suit

and tie and when he asks a suspect a question that he already knows the answer to, he tugs on his ear. I am thinking about this because I look over at Wade leaning against the bar and see that now he is tugging at his ear, too. And Goran also almost always has one or two days beard on his face because, like Wade, he's too busy thinking about things to think about shaving.

There's a lot going on here tonight at The Tavern, what with the bar stools all full of girls in skirts that are too tight and too short and whose legs don't touch the ground so when they try and cross them over and over again, back and forth, you can almost see their underwear and the Shores guys with pot bellies leaning over and trying to buy them drinks. If Goran were here, he'd be seeing more than what me and Wade see together, but I keep looking anyway, in between bites of these mozzarella sticks I am dipping in marinara I'm pretty sure is left over from Pasta Night. Everyone's all smiles on Ladies Night, the women to each other and to the men, the men to the women. There's a young kid named Ricky sitting on a bar stool in the corner playing the guitar and singing old songs his parents must have taught him, like *You've Got a Friend* and *Bad Bad Leroy Brown* and every once in a while, a guy pulls a girl off her barstool and starts waltzing her around the small space between the stools and the dining room tables.

I don't think Roberta ever missed a Ladies Night while she was alive. Now I wonder if Sam Billings had ever been in here on a Thursday night

and I stare at the men who are here a little more
carefully. If Sam Billings had stopped into The
Tavern on a Ladies Night, maybe on his way home
from a meeting or something, he'd of seen Roberta
in her high heels and shorts in the summer twirling
around on a barstool or dancing with one of her
girlfriends. He'd of thought 'now there's one good-
looking woman' because that's what almost all the
men said about Roberta when she was alive. But at
least she had the good sense not to dance with any
man while Wade was leaning at the edge of the bar,
arms folded across his chest and watching all the
goings on.

When Crystal brings me my second appetizer,
a big basket of popcorn shrimp, I ask her, "How's
Wade doing these days?"

"Oh, you know," she says, "ok, I guess. He's
pretty quiet, Wade. Doesn't say much." She almost
looks like she's blushing when she says this but then
with all these people in here tonight, it's pretty hot.

"Never did," I say and she says, "No, but even
less now."

I don't need to get into a contest about who
knows best how quiet Wade is so I just nod my
head. My husband was not the quiet type at all.
When he drove me home from the hospital, he was
yelling what the hell was I going to do now because
all that glass and the stitches left scars on my face
and he wanted to know just who was going to let
me be around customers looking like I did. He said,
it's a grocery store, for Chrissakes, Belle. Who's
gonna be able to look at you when they're buying

their food?

He was always worried about money, my
husband, even though we lived in the house I grew
up in and that my father had all paid for and that
my mother left me when she died. What're we
gonna do for money, he wanted to know because
even though he worked at a gas station, we couldn't
make it on just what he made, at least not with his
going out every single night and spending what we
had. I said I'd bet Publix would find me another
job in the store, in the back or in the office, or
maybe I'd get another job, maybe even at a hospital
where people wouldn't be so surprised by me, but
I'd check with Publix first because they'd been
good to me and I was a good worker. But he just
kept shaking his head and asking me why I was so
clumsy, how could I have been so stupid, and taking
the corners too quick and now I wonder what
would have happened if we had lived anywhere
near a canal. He was driving way faster than I
would have liked him to, like he just couldn't wait
to get home.

As soon as he set me on the couch, he went
upstairs to take a shower, to get the hospital smell
off him he said. I laid down and the next thing I
knew, I woke up and it was dark and he was gone.
I don't mean gone for the night like usual, I mean
gone. Just like that. And I did have a lot of scars
then and I still have them but they're real faded and
just like little lines now here and there on my face
and neck and I grew some bangs to cover the ones
on my forehead. What my husband didn't know

and didn't stick around to find out was that Publix
said I could go on disability because when I fell off
their old broken ladder, my ankle broke in three
places and the doctors said it would never be the
same so I couldn't stand for a long time or walk
around the store picking things up and putting
them away and I sure couldn't get up on any ladder
anymore. So one day I was a married lady with a
decent face and a good smile and a good job and
then the next day I'm all by myself and I don't even
look like myself and I have nowhere to go. But I
grew into this life and I want to tell Wade that he
will too. I never found out where my husband went
and I know that's better than knowing your wife
drowned in a canal holding hands with some man
you never knew but eventually I stopped wondering
and Wade will, too. But in the meantime, I want to
help him try to get some more answers because I
know how bad I wanted some in the beginning.

On Friday mornings I go to the bank to deposit
my checks and then to the post office to pay my
bills. I can walk everywhere in the Shores if I take
my cane so I do my errands on foot but then I come
home and get in my car and drive to the turnpike.
The more I go there, the more I think about how
much I don't know. When I'm not watching **Law
& Order** reruns, I am a sucker for old movies,
especially the kind where someone gets in an
accident or gets a terminal illness and has to die. I
like romance. I like the way people get sick in the
movies, the way they lay in bed under the covers
and smile like they know something they didn't

know before. The person they're leaving knows
they're dying and before they die, that person leans
over and gives them this sad kind of kiss on the
cheek. It's the kind of kiss that says if you could still
live, I'd do everything different. I think some people
deserve that chance and I like the movies best when
they all get to have that chance, when the smiling
dying person comes back to life from that kiss on
the cheek. I imagine Roberta had a smile like that
when, holding Sam Billings's hand, she knew that
her car was going under the water in the canal.
Her smile didn't work like it does in the movies
sometimes, I guess, but I wonder what she knew
then. I bet Goran would know.

I get to The Tavern early on Friday because
"Fish Fry" is the most popular dinner and if you
get there too late, you have to wait for a table. Also
if you have to wait too long for your order, the oil
they fry the fish in gets dark and metal tasting and
the fish isn't as good. So I am there around 4:30,
just when it starts, and Clara's on and she just keeps
bringing me fish and tartar sauce and French fries
and hushpuppies until I tell her it's enough.

"You full, honey?" Clara says. She's older than
me and Crystal, maybe in her fifties, and sweet
as they come. I say, "Nope. Just done," because
that's what's true. I always know when I've had
enough and I think everyone does but still there's
some people who even when they know they've
had enough keep going and going until they make
themselves sick and then get lost in feeling like
they're going to be sick, they're that full of it all,

that sick.

"Seen the paper today?" Clara asks me when she sets down the coffee.

"No," I say, "how come? Good coupons?" Clara is always telling me about the bargains.

"Well, sure, always on Friday but that's not it. Article about Roberta and that Sam Billings. Seems they had a kid."

"What?" I say. "What do you mean they had a kid? What kind of kid?"

"Crazy one, I guess. Go home and read your paper, Belle," she says. "They had a kid. In a mental house."

There are four **Law & Order** reruns on in a row and even a new one on Channel 6 but I read the article about Roberta and Sam Billings and their kid over and over again and never even turn on the TV. I don't get my ice cream, either. There's a picture of Roberta that is her high school yearbook picture, where she's the Circleville Pumpkin Queen; when I knew her, she looked good but she hadn't looked this good in years but then right next to it is a picture of a kid, eight years old it said, who has Roberta's same squinty eyes, round cheeks and puggy pig nose. Roberta was pretty even with those eyes and that nose and this little girl is pretty too except you can see there's something wrong with her, that she's what they call slow. It's in the way she is looking at the camera. She's not all there. And there's a picture of Sam Billings too and you can see the girl has Sam Billings' curly hair.

According to the paper, Wade was cleaning out

Roberta's closet and he found this big winter coat stuck in the way back. No one needs a big winter coat in Miami, even in January when sometimes it gets cold. But you do need one up in north Florida, like in Gainesville where the big college is and also the home for slow kids like Roberta and Sam Billings' slow kid.

The coat pockets were full of Polaroid pictures, pictures of Roberta and Sam Billings and their kid. There were letters, too, that the paper said were written by a nurse but from the kid to her parents saying Dear Mama and Daddy, I love you and I miss you and I like when you bring me the candy. The reporter said that also in the pockets were empty candy wrappers all balled up, Milky Ways and licorice and Twix. When Wade found these things, he took them to the police because now he knew there was a kid in a mental house in Gainsville who didn't have any parents.

The kid's name was Amanda and the letters were signed "Love, Mandy" and they were on stationery from the hospital where Mandy lived. The paper said when Sam Billings' wife found out about her husband's kid with Roberta, she said she knew the exact day that child was born because eight years ago, she'd had her appendix out in an emergency and no one could find Sam but then he showed up in her hospital room the next morning in the same clothes he'd had on the morning before when he said he was going to work. He kissed his wife and then shook her doctor's hand and on his wrist was one of those bracelets they give new fathers in the maternity ward.

"He was too tired not to be a moron, I guess" Mrs. Billings was quoted as saying in the paper. "He was there at that same hospital all night. With me having my appendix out and him having a retarded baby."

That party for Wade and Roberta's wedding was on a Saturday night and I guess now we know that Roberta and Sam Billing's Mandy was born about a year before. But now there's even more that we don't know.

For me, Saturday is the longest day of the week. I don't have any errands to do and I don't like to shop then because the stores are all so crowded with people who have to work all week and can't get to the stores except on Saturdays. On Sundays I take a long time to read the big paper and I go to church and spend the day resting until supper time when I go to The Tavern, but on Saturdays I just don't have that much to do. I drink some coffee at my kitchen table and eat some toast and then I straighten up my house but it doesn't take long because it's just me here and I'm pretty neat. Then I go out to my little yard and pick a few weeds and then I go back inside to cool off. I don't drive out to the turnpike on Saturdays or Sundays because those are days when a lot of people go to memorials and to pay respects or just take a leisurely drive and I like to keep what I'm doing private. During the week, people are driving the turnpike so fast to get to their work or wherever they're going, that they don't even look up when I'm out by the spot where

Roberta and Sam Billings drove off the road but
Saturdays and Sundays are different, more slow. So
on Saturday I water my plants and take a nap and
look through the paper for deals to tell Clara about
when she comes in on the next Friday and check
to see if I need milk or stamps for when I run my
errands on Monday and dust a little more and then
see if I can find anything on the TV. I do all this
until it's finally 5:00 and I can go to The Tavern for
supper. Saturday night is Wings Night and I can eat
my weight in wings.

I take my usual seat and look around for Wade.
Crystal comes to my table and says "Ready for your
first round of wings" and I'm about to say yes when
for some reason tonight I say, "Not just yet. Bring
me a cocktail, Crystal," and she says, "A cocktail?
Well, la-de-dah, Belle. What, you celebrating
something?" and I say, "Sure, I'm celebrating
Saturday night. I'll have a Whiskey Sour" and
Crystal goes off to get it. I plant my feet more firmly
on the floor and pull the table closer to my chest.
I'm not much of a drinker and one Whiskey Sour
will do something to me so I want to be stable.

"Wade around?" I ask, when Crystal sets my
drink down. It's a light orangey color in a tall
skinny glass and there's a cherry and an orange slice
on a plastic toothpick floating in it. I pull it out and
eat the orange and think I will not try to tie a knot
in the cherry stem with my tongue.

"He is," Crystal says, "in the kitchen. Says he's
not coming out too much tonight. Too many people
read that article in the paper about Roberta's kid.

You read it?"

"I did," I say, "and will you tell Wade I need to talk to him. Just for a minute."

"Sure I will," Crystal says, "he'll come out for you. You're our best customer, Belle. Like family."

"Sure I am," I say. I eat my dinner in The Tavern every night.

A few sips of the Whiskey Sour later, Wade comes out and heads directly to my table. He's wearing a Miami Dolphins t-shirt and some jeans that look old.

"How you doing, Belle?" he says.

"I'm doing good, Wade. How you doing?"

"Good, I'm good," he says. "Mind if I sit down?" and he sits down.

"Can I buy you a drink?" I ask but he tells me no, he can't sit too long. "Gotta lot a wings to fry up tonight." I see what he means because The Tavern is starting to fill up with customers, more customers than usual at this hour it seems.

"So Crystal says you wanna talk to me?" and I say I do.

"If it's about that stuff in the paper, Belle, well, you know, I just don't really want to talk much about that."

"Well, it is and it isn't," I say. This is one of those nights again when Wade hasn't shaved so he's got stubble all around his chin and of course it reminds me of Goran. **Law & Order's** a TV show, I know, but now I think Wade is a lot like Goran, so busy thinking all the time and trying to figure things out that it doesn't occur to him to think about what he's wearing or to shave. And I think that's what's been going on with Wade all this time I've known him and maybe longer. And especially now. And I think all of a sudden that I understand Detective Eames better than I ever have before and that even though Wade is smart, he needs a little help now.

"You know I was at the turnpike the other day, where Roberta went over?" I say and he says "Belle" like a warning but I put my hand up to show I need to go on. "And there's some flowers planted there now and a wooden cross."

"What are you saying, Belle?' Wade asks me.

"I'm saying that there's still some things happening there, things that could be clues."

Wade puts his forehead in his hand and looks down at the table. He's shaking his head. "That's nice, Belle, that's fine," he says, "but I don't need no clues. I know what happened." Then he picks his head up and looks around his restaurant, maybe to see how many of his customers know what happened, too.

"But not why they went over into the canal, Wade," I say. "There's no one who's figured that out. They had a kid and so..."

"...so they were going to see her," he says, "that night. That's it. Like they did every Friday night, I guess, except I didn't know it."

"Well, where did you think she was then, on those Friday nights?" I asked this question like I am a detective, but it is also something I've always wanted to know.

"Out. With her girlfriends. She hated Fish Fry

Night, thought it stunk up the place and me, too.
Smell on my clothes. I even thought about changing
the fish fry to pizza or tacos or something. But I
didn't ever think about it hard enough, I guess."

In all these years that I've known Wade, I never
heard him talk so much. I push my Whiskey Sour
to him and when he picks it up and takes a big
drink, I know my instincts are good. If anyone in
The Tavern who doesn't know us sees us, they're
going to think that me and Wade are a married
couple, having a talk and sharing a drink. I wonder
if, secretly, Goran and Eames are in love and I
don't see why not. Neither one is married—at least
they never talk about being married and I've seen
every episode over and over again. They're partners
and friends and they are good together. He figures
things out and so can she but she admires him and
looks after him and knows he's got a special kind
of mind, one you can't predict except to predict
that it will always be right. I look over at Wade and
think to myself Why not?, something I think I must
have been thinking about a long time but didn't
know until just at this minute. Maybe I was missing
something all along and it took Roberta and Sam
Billings going into the canal for me to finally figure
it out.

"Well, Wade," I say, "maybe you didn't know
what Roberta was doing and maybe, well yeah I
guess it's true, maybe it is so that Roberta lied but
you know something, Wade? Evidence doesn't lie." I
learned this from Goran. "Now there's flowers and
a cross at the spot on the turnpike and who knows,

maybe there's more stuff and I have a lot of free time and I could go, see what I could see."

"I've seen all I need to see, Belle," he says. He looks around the dining room, catches Crystal's eye and signals her over. While Crystal is walking to my table, she's tucking her shirt tighter into her skirt and smoothing some hair that has come out of her barrette. She's blushing, again, and suddenly I realize that now I know something else. I am a good detective. Wade finishes my drink.

"Bring Belle here another drink, on the house," he says, then he stands up. "Give her her dinner on the house tonight, too, all the wings she can eat." Crystal nods and pats me on the shoulder. Then he looks at me real seriously and it seems like he is seeing something he never saw before, too.

"In fact," he says, "from now on, give Belle all her dinners on the house every night." Then he turns to me and says, "You're a loyal customer, Belle, the most loyal one we got. That counts for something. You stick around. You know when something's good, I guess."

"I know a lot of things, Wade," I say, thinking I am a match for Goran now for sure.

"I guess you do, Belle," he says.

Then he bends over and kisses me on the cheek.

"That's sweet," I hear Crystal say but I am looking up at Wade and smiling the kind of smile that you see in the old movies, the kind that spreads and then right away starts to get smaller. It fades and gets thin because the person smiling it knows a lot of things. It's the way you see the dying smile, in the romantic movies on TV. But I know more now than I have ever known before so when Wade makes his way back to the kitchen, I look up at Crystal—sad Crystal who can stop tucking in her shirt now and smoothing her hair back—because sometimes a lifetime of loyalty is just the beginning of something else.

The Butcher

"You love Jesus?" the woman screamed when she pulled up beside Janine on Alton Road. "You tryin' to meet him?"

Janine was driving home from the grocery store thinking about how much longer her aunt might live, how much longer she might live with her aunt and she had unknowingly drifted into the woman's lane. Quickly, she moved back over.

"Hey, Jesus lover, I'm talkin' to you." Janine was driving her aunt's van that had a Jesus fish on the bumper.

There was a lot of traffic on Alton Road and it was moving slowly so Janine could not find a way to get away from the woman she had cut off. Janine turned to look at the woman and mouthed 'sorry' but she was more than that.

"Yeah, you're sorry all right," the woman said. She was old but trying to look young with a tube top that did not hold up her breasts, long white hair in pig tails, and sunglasses. She reminded Janine simultaneously of her mother—who made Janine help her bleach her hair and tie her halter tops—and her high school English teacher, a harsh woman who wore dark glasses indoors. Janine always had a hard time looking at her mother and she avoided looking at Mrs. Bell because she could not see her eyes.

"Here, you wanna meet Jesus? I'll help ya," the woman yelled and swerved her car so close to the van that if Janine had not turned right on 10th Street, the woman would have hit her.

At home, Janine was still feeling faint as she put the groceries away. She sat down for a few minutes before heating up some soup. The outside world was a difficult place for Janine; the unexpected often nearly did her in and negotiating the familiar, like this incident, left her short of breath and shaky. People in Miami were impatient, self-righteous, entitled and often crazy—especially on the road, where Janine navigated the big gray van as if it was a recalcitrant beast. Sometimes Janine woke up in the middle of the night to escape dreams of horns blasting, people swearing, the van veering, brakes slamming. More often than not, she couldn't fall asleep again and stayed up until the sun rose, thinking of ways she could run her errands on foot.

"Are you back?" her aunt called from the bedroom, where she was propped up and watching "Days of Our Lives."

The days of Janine's life were taken up with daily trips to the grocery and cooking food her aunt could not eat.

"Yes, Tia, I'm back," Janine called.

"What kind of pudding did you get today?"

"Banana."

Tia had cancer and six weeks ago, at the end of May, her doctor had said she probably only had weeks to live; Janine wanted to make her aunt's last days as comfortable as possible and to give back something invaluable that she had gotten: on her sixteenth birthday, Janine's father left and two days later her furious mother had packed up and moved to Atlanta so Janine had moved in with Tia. But now it was mid-July and although Tia was weak and ill and eighty-six years old, it did not seem to Janine that her aunt would actually die, mostly because Tia was not at all afraid to die. She did not feel alone and was not afraid of anything, including meeting Jesus.

"I am ready for the Lord when He is ready for me," Tia always said. She was a devoted Catholic who had gone to church every morning before she got sick. Faith and lack of fear seemed to give Tia strength and stamina; everything was easy--living, dying, believing in God. Janine loved her and studied her for clues to her courage and her calm.

"You need to eat the soup before the pudding, Tia," Janine said with the same authority she used in her job as a Kindergarten aide. Tia's doctor had said that although she would not be able to eat much, she should be able to have whatever she wanted. But what she wanted were the foods she could not eat—steaks, chops, roasts, pork loins. Tia loved meat but she could barely digest scrambled eggs. Still, she wanted to listen to and smell a hamburger sizzling in a pan, to touch a finger to a salted roast and taste the drippings, to see the red juices leave a perfectly grilled steak. Janine had never learned how to cook so she went to the library and took out cookbooks and followed the directions for cooking every kind of meat, and some things Tia actually could eat.

Tia stuck a spoon into the soup and said, "Cream

of Potato?" and when Janine said yes, her aunt said, "next time add oregano and it will taste homemade."

Janine nodded her head. The soup was homemade. "What's happening on the soap opera?"

"Oh, you know, these people," Tia said, shaking her spoon at the television, "the same thing every day. You think they would learn. They want to kill each other, have sex with everyone, with strangers. They love each other, they hate each other...that one?" and she pointed to a young blonde girl on the screen, "she had sex with her own brother and didn't even know it. And all the screaming..."

"I got screamed at today," Janine blurted out.

"You got screamed at? You're such a good girl. Who would scream at you?"

"A woman on Alton Road. I cut her off accidentally. She asked me if I wanted to meet Jesus."

"Well, of course you do. What kind of a question is that?"

For the last couple of weeks, Father MacMahon had been coming over in the afternoons to say the mass with Tia. Janine would make him tea and sit there with them while they prayed, listening intently and then waiting for the chance to say, more tea, Father? Do you like those cookies, Father?

"She saw the Jesus fish on the van."

"Well, of course you want to meet Jesus. Did you tell her?"

"Sure Tia, I told her," Janine lied. She was as afraid of meeting Jesus as she was of everything else.

"Look, Jannie, look there," Tia was pointing at the television again. "That's Marlena. Sometimes she's possessed by the devil."

She needs to meet Jesus, Janine thought. She began to fidget, to stir Tia's soup that wasn't being eaten.

"What's the matter with you?" Tia asked.

"I'm just so nervous in the van, Tia. It's so big and I get in people's way."

"Don't let this crazy woman rattle you, dear."

"It's not just her. People always say things to me, things about Jesus because of the fish on the bumper. And the van is so big. Maybe I should see if I can drive Daddy's car."

"You learned how to drive in that van, Janine."

"I know. But the streets are too crowded now and it's hard. I think I'll see if the Fiesta will start."

"Go shopping at night," Tia said.

Janine was sure she misunderstood her aunt so she said, "So it's all right?"

"No. Your father's car hasn't been started since the day he left. You drive the van. But you'll go at night. Like I used to."

"At night?" Janine felt her pulse quicken.

"Sure," Tia said, "I'd set my alarm for 2 or 3 in the morning and go then. It's nice at the store then, not so many people, and you get better service. I did it for years until I got sick, the whole time you've been here with me and you never knew I was gone. The meat is fresher, no one's been poking it because the people who shop in the middle of the night, they don't want meat...they like chips and frozen pizza and beer. And there's less people on the road to honk and scream at you. Go at night, Jannie. That's the best thing."

"You went to the store in the middle of the

night?"

"You go at night," Tia said, ignoring her. "Try it. You'll see. It's better."

If there was one thing Janine knew, it was that she would never be able to get herself to go out in the middle of the night. She said, "It's time for your nap."

"Wake me when the Father comes."

"Don't I always?"

Father MacMahon was old but ageless. He still had a full head of dark black hair which Janine suspected he dyed and she envied him his vanity. His hands were large and always warm and when Tia took both of them in her bony cold ones, she pulled them up to her chin and smelled them, as if she was clasping a bouquet. Janine loved the way Tia lit up when she opened her eyes from her nap and saw the Father standing at her bed. She loved the way he accepted the hot mug of tea, with a benevolent bending of his head like a blessing. She loved calling him Father.

Janine turned the television off and took the tray from Tia's lap. In the kitchen while doing the dishes, she found herself back in the van and hearing the woman with the pigtails and sunglasses yelling at her. Driving the big van was too hard. And many times the grocery shopping was as bad as the driving—the aisles were as crowded as the streets and people bumped her cart and rolled their eyes and tried to push her out of their way. Even when she was just standing still and someone came around an aisle too fast and smacked their cart into hers, her face would get hot and red and her neck would start to hurt, like whiplash, and she'd have to realign herself, all the while apologizing to someone who had run into her and was now halfway down the aisle. But she could not stop herself from apologizing because she believed, in a profound way, that these incidents were her fault. Although young, naïve, and absurdly inexperienced at 22, there were some deep solid facts Janine knew about the world. It was dangerous, unpredictable, explosive and if you were not careful, as Janine had once not been careful, you could be responsible for an irreversible act.

When Father MacMahon arrived, he gently tapped Tia who took his hands immediately so Janine set the mug of tea down on an end table. She had another banana pudding for Tia and some gingersnaps for the Father. While Tia and the Father prayed, Janine sat at the foot of the bed and marveled at their faith. When Janine's mother had moved to Atlanta, she had taken the bus. Janine did not know how her father got to wherever he was going, since he left Janine his car, not realizing that she would never be able to bring herself to get inside it once he was gone. For months after Tia had taught her how to drive in the big gray van, she had driven it around the city looking for him. She had prayed continuously that he would come home. When neither or those activities produced results, she fell asleep willing her spirit into the red Ford Fiesta and woke up having dreamt of herself driving the car because she believed it could find him. He was a traveling salesman: he spent most of his life in that car.

Father MacMahon declined the daily dinner invitation Janine offered and when he left and she

had done up the tea cups and cookie plate, she set
a marinated flank steak on a hot grill pan and then
turned to the cupboards for something Tia could
eat. She chose Cream of Wheat. Stirring it, she
wondered if the Father knew how long Tia might
live, if perhaps Jesus had told him a secret. The
doctors didn't know: they were amazed at her aunt's
stamina. Janine did not want Tia to die because she
loved her and she loved living there, taking care of
her aunt, having a purpose that was so much more
focused and important than the work she did at the
elementary school. At the school, she took children to
the bathroom, set out cookies and juice, cleaned up
finger paint, paste they had flung, painted macaroni
and Popsicle sticks from the floor, and put everything
away at the end of the day. But Tia needed her to live.
There were six weeks before school would start again.
Janine wondered what would happen in late August,
how much longer they both had.

Tia put her whole small face as close to the flank
steak as she could and breathed in as deeply as her
weary lungs would let her. Then she opened her
mouth and licked the top of the steak.

"Nice, honey, nice work," she said. "Your uncle
used to chop this steak and put it in a pot with
tomatoes and peppers and onions...I made some rice.
But now I think noodles would have been good, too."

"Noodles would have been good," Janine said,
spooning up a mouthful of Cream of Wheat. "So is
this," she said, pushing the spoon toward her aunt's
greasy mouth.

"I can feed myself," Tia said.

"But you don't" Janine said, and Tia let her slide the cereal in.

"What's the point? I'm not hungry for anything besides this steak."

"Well, what do you want tomorrow? What can I make you that you would want to eat?"

Tia struggled to swallow the Cream of Wheat and signaled to Janine for water. The water was warm; it helped Tia get the food down.

"Liver," she said, once she'd swallowed. "Yeah, liver I want."

"Liver?" Janine's memory of liver was an awful smell and a tough consistency that no amount of threats from her mother could make her eat.

"Chicken livers...you cook them and then put them in the grinder and make them smooth. I could eat those...they're smooth like this," and Tia pointed to the cereal.

"All right then," Janine said, "chicken livers it is. I'll get them tomorrow."

"You'll get them tonight."

* * *

At 2:00 in the morning, Tia called out and Janine woke up, the baseball bat she slept with in her hand.

"What, Tia? What is it?" Janine said, running to her aunt's room. She was panicked and her heart was a cyclone in her chest. Tia could be calling out for water or for the cool wash cloth she liked when she couldn't sleep or she could be calling out because her breath was coming too fast and maybe she was ready to go and Janine knew all of this, but she also knew that Tia could be calling out for something else—

something very wrong—and that if she had to, Janine could wield the bat into someone's head or gut with the power she had been helpless to access once before.

"What is it, Tia?" she said, coming into her aunt's room. She turned the light on and saw nothing but her aunt squinting, putting a hand up to cover her eyes.

"So bright," Tia said, squinting. Then moving her hand and getting adjusted to the light, she saw the bat. "Oh, honey," she said with a sigh.

Janine let the bat drop to her side. "What's the matter, Tia? Why are you up?" she said.

"Time to go to the store," Tia said.

Janine sat down at the foot of Tia's bed and tried every rational protest she could think of and then, when none of her excuses worked, she finally told the truth. "I can't leave the house now."

Tia shook her head.

"I can't go out at night, Tia. Especially not now, in the middle of the night."

Tia did not respond. Then Janine tried something else. "What if you need me?"

"What I need," Tia said, "is chicken livers, and to know that when I leave you for good, you will know that you can do some things you never thought you could do. Get dressed. Get the van. Go to the store. You'll see."

The only thing Janine was more used to than fear was obediency and by 2:30, she was at the store.

Nighttime at the grocery store was so different than daytime at the grocery store that Janine walked in with her cart and then didn't seem to know what to do. Normally, she went directly to produce, got vegetables she could mash or stew, went to dairy, canned goods, things she needed for cleaning and then finally to meats. But when she walked in at 2:30 in the morning and saw that most of the cashier stations were empty, that there were no people to dodge or stand behind while they compared brands of soap, that there was no line at the coffee machine and the deli was half dark, she had to stand still for a few minutes to get her bearings.

Even the nighttime grocery store music was different; she recognized an old Eagles song she didn't even know she knew: you can't hide your lying eyes. It reminded her of the woman who yelled at her on Alton Road, the woman with the dark glasses whose eyes she couldn't see. You tryin' to meet Jesus? Not tonight, Janine thought. She had a feeling she couldn't identify at first and then realized it was surprise but not the kind she was used to, the kind that made her blink and shudder; this one had a kind of solidity to it, an anchoring. It felt good. She went to get the chicken livers.

The day butcher was a young guy who winked at the attractive customers and was good at getting them to buy more meat than they had on their lists but he never paid any attention to Janine. She saw him flirt with ladies who lingered over meat selections and his attentions. On rare occasions when Janine couldn't find something specific Tia had suggested—beef short ribs or, once, a special kind of Italian sausage—timidly, she asked him for help but he always appeared annoyed by her questions. He flicked his finger in some vague direction and Janine, in the end, was too

shy to ask again and had to find the item herself. But
it did not matter: the young butcher reminded Janine
of the boys she had learned to ignore in high school,
the ones who called her Kraft Single and who called
her two best friends Pepperidge and Farm—the two
fat girls the bread and the overly thin Janine nothing
more than a slice of processed cheese. Petra and
Lulu would call them names and Janine would try to
ssshhh them, to stop them before something worse
than name-calling could happen. But nothing ever
happened and the three girls survived high school with
nothing more serious than humiliation. Now Petra
lived in Orlando with her husband, a man twice her
age her mother had found for her at church, and Lulu
had moved to Key West to help her brother open a t-
shirt store. Janine missed them, her two best and only
friends, almost as much as she missed her father.

The night butcher was an older man, Janine's
father's age, and resembled him in a vague way:
he was short, balding, and was trying to grow a
moustache. Janine's father had been on the road every
week and when he would come home on Friday
nights, he would have a day or two of beard growth
on his face. Janine met him on the corner every Friday
night at 9:00. She got through the terror of being
in the elevator alone at night by replacing what she
thought could happen to her in there—fire, assault,
even just getting stuck—with thoughts that came true:
moments alone with her father when he arrived.

They lived in a nice neighborhood that bordered
a neighborhood with a bad reputation and Janine
would stand in the dark doorway watching for

criminals and for the red Ford Fiesta to turn down
the street. By the time it pulled into its parking space,
Janine would be running to the curb. She would get
a great bear hug from her father, and more. In the
elevator on the way up to their apartment, Janine felt
safe and warm and always excited because her father
would have one arm around her shoulder and with
the other, he'd pull out whatever he had brought his
daughter that week—a hair clip with sparkles, fancy
chocolates, a package of different sized paper clips in
neon colors. As she got older, a tape of a new band he
had heard of while he was on the road, a gift card to a
teen clothing store, a real pink sapphire ring, a fat cute
stuffed cow, pens, pencils, rulers with the names of
towns he'd been, ball caps, t-shirts, one time a savings
bond—though her mother took that as soon as she
saw it.

Once in the apartment, her father would sink
down into the couch and while her mother started in
on him about bills, about things she wanted that she
never had enough money to buy, about parties she
hadn't been able to go to because he was never home,
Janine would be sitting next to him, leaning into his
soft shoulder and examining what he had brought
her. Sitting there, Janine could feel her father's limp
exhaustion through his rolled up shirt sleeves and then
she could feel it harden into the tension her mother's
assault always produced.

Every week for as long as Janine could remember,
her father came home on Friday night with a will to
withstand his wife's berating and a special gift for
his daughter. And then on her sixteenth birthday, he

didn't come home at all. When Janine got downstairs, she saw his car already at the curb but when she got to it, it was empty. There was a red ribbon tied to the windshield.

The night butcher seemed very intent on his work. He wore a white apron over his shirt but you could still see some chest hair peeking out because he had not buttoned his shirt all the way up. Around his neck was a thick gold rope chain. Janine's father never wore jewelry, not even his wedding ring. But this man was older than the daytime butcher and looked wiser, more serious, and Janine was feeling euphoric about being at the grocery store at night so she approached him.

"Excuse me," Janine said to the butcher; she had no idea where chicken livers would be.

"Hello, Beauty," he said. "how can I help you?"

Janine swallowed hard. Her euphoria dissolved into the familiarity of fearing strangers. The night of the robbery, she waited for the elevator that would take her to her father but when the doors opened and she said excuse me to the two men who were coming out as she was trying to get in, they had grabbed her and pushed her back into the apartment. The robbers had called her "baby" which at the moment sounded too much like "beauty."

She opened her mouth but did not speak.

"Help. How I help you?" the butcher asked and when he did, Janine saw that he was looking at her neck. Memories she had been trying to repress for six years kicked in as did her flight response, the same one she had when she found herself shoved back into her

own home with two strangers staring hard at her. She
was about to turn away when the butcher said, "you
need meat, no? What you need?"

I need to go, Janine thought. But then she
remembered Tia, remembered the only reason why
she was there in the middle of the night.

"Chicken livers," Janine said.

"Ah, right here," he said and turning toward the
shelving behind him, walked over and pointed to a
grouping of plastic containers.

There were varying amounts in each container
and she selected the smallest one. She was about to
utter "thank you" when the butcher said, "They are
fresh. I take them from the chickens tonight myself."

That couldn't be true, Janine thought, but she was
too unnerved to say anything. The little butcher was
still standing next to her, so close she could smell the
fruity scent from the gum he was chewing.

"No, I don't" he said, laughing, "but they are
fresh."

"Thank you," Janine finally said, and turned to
walk away.

"So your husband, he likes the livers from
chickens, no?" the butcher said.

"No," Janine said.

"He no like them? Then why you get them?"

"No, I mean I'm not married," Janine answered.

"What?" He stepped back in fake alarm. "You not
married? A beautiful woman like you?"

Janine was a girl, not a woman. She looked down
at her feet and then into her cart, empty but for a
carton of chicken livers.

"I have to go," she said and as she walked away, she heard the butcher say, "I not believe this. Beauty like you."

In high school, there were ordinary girls and there were extraordinary girls and nearly all of them had boyfriends. Janine was a plain girl, a girl of average height and not much weight with long thin hair the color of dull light who had never even been invited to a party. She and Petra and Lulu went to the mall or the movies or McDonalds and after they moved away, Janine did not know where to meet new friends. At the school where she worked, most everyone was older than she was and married and the young single teachers never said anything to her beyond Hello. She was invisible. Her eyes were a pale gray and her eyebrows were the same color as her hair and in too much Miami Beach sun, she nearly faded out of sight. She had never been on a date and other than one of the robber's parting jokes, she had never been kissed.

While Janine headed toward the van in the parking garage, whatever courage she had felt when she first got to the store had vanished. Now she just felt a familiar looming sense of danger: the butcher had been too friendly, too familiar. Finally she reached the van. But just as she was about to get in, a car that seemed to come out of nowhere screeched to a stop behind her, making real the terror she had only imagined a second before.

"Jesus rocks."

Janine turned to see a car full of teenagers behind her. They were only a few years younger than she was but suddenly she felt like an old woman. Her knees began to shake and she pressed her hand against the driver's side door for support.

"The Lord is so cool," a girl in the back seat said.

It was almost 3:00 in the morning. Janine tried to grab the door handle but her palms were wet with nervous sweat and her hand slipped off. She tried it again, faster, unable to grasp it or to erase the image of one of the robber's fists slamming into her father's jaw when they discovered he had only $53 in his pocket, and a University of Florida key chain wrapped in tissue for his daughter.

"Praise the Lord, man, and the fish," the driver said. "Jesus is King."

Janine heard a shriek in her head saying "you wanna meet him?" but it was in her mother's voice and then it was screaming "what do you want?" but then that was in her own voice.

"Nothing, man, just your parking space," the driver said. There were dozens of empty parking spaces in the lot. Janine wiped her hand on her jeans and quickly got into the van. She backed out and as the teenagers pulled in, she saw a Jesus fish on their bumper.

* * *

"So, you like the store at night, eh?" Tia asked in the morning when Janine brought her some oatmeal and some tea. "The meat is nice, right?"

"The meat is fine," Janine said. She did not want to think about the store at night.

"What's this?" Tia asked. "Peppermint tea?" She took a sip and crinkled her nose. "I miss coffee. How about a little coffee tomorrow?"

"You're not supposed to have coffee, Tia. You know that."

"And you're not supposed to be spending your summer off making slop for an old woman."

"I love taking care of you."

"I know you do, Jannie," Tia said, with a sigh, "but it's not what you're supposed to do. It won't be much longer now, I know. So bring me some coffee tomorrow, ok?"

Janine looked at her aunt and felt certain that Tia knew something no one else could know. The doctors certainly didn't know.

"You know what?' she said, "you can have whatever you want. How about some coffee right now? I can make a pot in five minutes."

"Good girl," Tia said, "make a big pot so we can save some for the Father. He loves coffee. Make it strong."

All this time Janine had been making the Father tea and he had been drinking it and smiling. She made a pot of very strong coffee and put it with two mugs on a tray. She would have some, too, to help her stay awake. She had been unable to sleep when she got home from the store for all the faces in her dreams— the smiling butcher, the devil, the teenage driver who looked like a rock 'n roll Jesus.

"That newscaster?" Tia said pointing to the television when Janine came into the room, "what do you think of her hair? That hair would look good on you."

The newscaster's hair was dark red and cut so that the bangs swayed just above her eyes and the rest just fluttered on her broad shoulders. It made her look competent, authoritative, and seductive.

Janine looked at the newscaster and wondered if her thin hair could even do that. She'd had the same long hair since she was a small child. She was about to tell Tia that when suddenly an image of the butcher appeared in her head: what he would say if she showed up in the grocery with new hair? Would he think she thought she was a beauty?

"No, Tia, I couldn't have that hair," she said.

"Why not? You could use a change," Tia said, taking a sip from her mug. "This coffee is heaven. Thank you, Jesus."

Then Janine said, "Jesus rocks."

"What did you say?"

Janine told Tia about the teenagers from the parking garage with the Jesus fish on their car.

"Well, Jesus does rock," Tia said, "and he'd better have coffee up there."

Neither Janine nor Tia took a nap because of the strong coffee. When Father MacMahon came, Janine gave him some and he drank it down quickly right after the praying. He had to hurry back to the church to meet with a young couple who were getting married.

"What you about, Janine?" the Father asked but he was looking at Tia; obviously, this was something they had talked about. "You should get out and meet a nice fellow. You're a young girl. You need to think about marriage."

The only thoughts Janine ever had about marriage was how hard it was on her kind easy-going father and how easy it was for her demanding unpleaseable mother to destroy it.

"That's right, you tell her, Father. She doesn't listen to me," Tia said. "A young girl like this, spending all day here in this sickness. She needs to go out, meet some people. Get a new haircut and go out with young people."

"We have some very nice young people at the church, Janine," Father MacMahon said, "some nice social groups or the coffee gathering after Mass? You come. I'll introduce you."

Before Janine could politely refuse, Tia said, "she'll be there. This Sunday. And in a dress."

Tia did know something Janine didn't know but it had little to do with how much longer she had to live. What she knew was that her niece did not know to live in the world she belonged to. Girls her age were carefree, vain, full of energy and bliss. They worked so they could buy clothes and make-up and shoes and were never home. Once it was clear that neither of Janine's parents were coming back, Tia had thought the best thing was to become both of those parents—to cook for Janine, teach her how to drive, watch television with her, tuck her in at night even though she was sixteen, to show her she could be safe again, and that she was loved. Tia thought if she was good at this, then eventually Janine would—like other girls her age—navigate herself back into her world. But she did not. Now Tia hoped that she would just have enough time to prepare Janine to live her own life and if that plan included meeting a nice Catholic boy at the coffee social after Mass, all the better. When she heard

Janine tell the Father goodbye and the door click shut, she called Janine back into her room.

"The Father is right: you need to meet some young people. You'll get a new haircut and a new dress. You'll go to the Church."

Janine still wore the clothes she'd had in high school. She said, "Well, right now I need to go clean the kitchen and you need to get some rest. Now lay back down."

Tia closed her eyes. "You'll go to church," she said softly.

"Sure, Tia," Janine said, and she turned out the light.

At 1:30 in the morning, Janine was wide awake and sitting straight up in bed. She didn't remember coming out of sleep but the image of a thick crowd of people she couldn't find her way through was still lurking in her mind. She must have been having another bad dream. Her legs ached, as if she had been trying to run, and she was breathing too fast. She went down to the kitchen to warm up some milk.

Tia had requested homemade chicken soup for lunch and supper so eventually Janine had to go to the store. Although the butcher had unnerved her and the harmless teenagers nearly made her faint, the quiet near-empty nighttime grocery store did have its appeal. And she had felt something there she couldn't remember ever having felt before. It was a kind of confidence and it, too, returned like a dream. She drank the milk and hoped for weariness but found herself more and more awake.

Maybe the butcher wouldn't be there. Or if he

was, maybe he wouldn't be near the whole chickens
so she could just pick one up quickly and head to
the cashier before he saw her. It took all day to make
chicken soup and would be so much easier if she
started in the middle of the night, especially since the
warm milk had no effect other than to make Janine
feel sweaty. She rinsed her glass in the sink and headed
toward the shower: she knew there was no way she
could go to church on Sunday and make small talk
with the people her age who congregated there but she
could take a deep breath and go to the grocery store.

"Ah, my midnight beauty." The butcher had
come up behind her. When she'd gotten to the meat
department, he was nowhere to be seen so she had no
idea where he had come from, how he had seen her.

"You're a night owl, like me, eh?' he said. This
time, his breath smelled of coffee and chocolate.

"It's just easier at night," she said, wondering why
she was explaining this to a man she did not want to
talk to. She put the chicken in her cart and turned to
leave.

"Everything easier in the night," he said winking.
Then she watched him look her up and down. She
wondered if her father, on his many travels, had ever
talked to young girls like this. In her memory, he was
a shy man, a man who winced when his wife shrieked,
who was not good at making eye contact, who didn't
really speak unless someone spoke to him first. Where
was he now? Was he talking to someone?

"Ah, away with the thoughts," the butcher
said. His English was broken and a combination of
standard phrases and idioms. "Well, here is another

thing from the thoughts: it is better even to come later.
Later at night. Here it is better then."

Janine looked at her watch. It was 2:15.

"Helping the customer, Harris?" A large man in a
white shirt and pants from a good suit had come up
behind them.

"Yessir, boss, no problems here at all, boss,"
Harris the butcher said.

"That's good, Harris. That's what I like to see,"
and he disappeared into the Employees Only door.

Harris moved closer to Janine.

"The boss, Gonzalez?" Harris pointed in the
direction of where the man had gone, "he wants that
I help you. You want that I help you?" Harris was
whispering and his chocolate breath traveled the air
Janine was inhaling. The sweetness was heavy and
lodged in her throat.

"I have what I need," she said in a whisper
because that was all the sound she could produce.

"Ah, it is the secret, yes? We whisper, yes," he said,
and then he pulled the chicken out of Janine's cart. "I
have what you need," he was still whispering and now
winking too and he reached for a different chicken.
"Take this one...it will make you a better soup." He
put the plumper bird in her cart.

"How did you know I was making soup?" she
said, her voice returning with her surprise.

Harris laughed. "Look, you have the carrot and
the onion and the turnip...you have the herbs, the
parsley, this..." and he held up a package of fresh dill,
something he seemed not to know the English word
for. "You have a fine time with this things."

Janine didn't know what to say.

"What? You think only the women know how to cook the soup?"

Sometimes on the weekends, Janine's father used to make a big pot of chili and they would sit in front of the television and eat it while her mother went out to bars with her friends. During the week, Janine's mother ordered take-out if she thought about eating at all.

"Si, of course, I make soup" Harris said, as if he was in a conversation with a customer instead of talking to a person who did not respond. "Chicken, tomato, tortilla..." He lifted the chicken back out of her cart. "I bet when you open up the chicken, you take all the neck and insides..." and he pointed to the plastic-wrapped gizzards and innards that came with every whole chicken, "and throw them away, eh?"

She did and so she nodded.

"Ah, well, I give you something, another secret." He leaned closer to Janine. "You put these in the pot, with the whole bird and then, after, you throw them away. Don't look afraid, they are just organs like you have." Harris reached out as if he was going to touch Janine just above the rim of her jeans but she stepped back before he could reach her. "Ha," he said laughing, "you are afraid of your own organs. But these here in this big girl," and he lifted the chicken up into the air, "they are what makes the best dish. If you can't look, close your eyes. Trust me."

He put the chicken back into her cart and she managed to say "ok" while putting her hands on the cart handle. She needed to get away.

"Now what, Beauty?" he asked.

"Now what?" she echoed.

"What else? What now?" he said.

She didn't know what else, what was supposed to happen now. She wished she had the newscaster's hair; then she would know what to do.

She turned to leave.

"Wait," Harris shouted, "wait here. I have something for you" and he disappeared behind the door Gonzalez the boss had gone through moments before.

Janine did not wait. She hurried to the check-out line and stood in the only one open at that hour.

There were two people in front of her and the cashier was taking her time ringing up the items. Janine thought she could just leave the groceries there in her cart and come back at 7:00 or 8:00, when she thought Harris's shift would be over. No one would notice. She could move her cart out of the line and then just leave. She felt her legs tingling, the anticipation of flight, but then she heard Harris's voice behind her.

"I find you," he said. "Here, take this. For you."

It was a white tulip, crafted out of a paper towel.

"Harris, leave the girls alone," the cashier said. Her nametag said Martina. "Haven't you learned your lesson?"

"You are jealous, Marti," Harris said, "because no one makes the flower for you. This one," and he pointed at Janine, "this one different. I know." Then he looked at Janine and said, "You won't take it? Here," and he set it on her purse in the cart.

Janine drove home very carefully even though there was very little traffic and all the stoplights were blinking yellow. The tulip was on the passenger's seat but Janine did not look at it.

By 4:30, the soup was bubbling and all the other groceries were put away. The chicken stock, darker and richer from the innards swirling around in it, released a warm comforting aroma that Janine's soup had never achieved. She sat down at the kitchen table to breathe it in when she heard Tia call her name.

Janine went to her aunt's room.

"I smell the soup," Tia said, leaning forward and staring at her niece. "But what's the matter with you? You're as jumpy as a cricket."

It was true but Janine hadn't even realized that her heart was beating too fast and her hands were shaking until her aunt said something. Janine had buried the paper tulip in the garbage can under the peelings of soup vegetables.

"Nothing...I just didn't expect you to be up. Why are you up? Why couldn't you sleep?"

"Sit down here, dear," Tia said, pointing to a spot on the bed next to her, "I've been doing some thinking and I want to talk to you."

Janine sat down on the bed and pulled the covers up around her aunt's neck. She could feel how ghostly thin Tia had gotten. When Tia lifted her arms and laid them on top of the covers, Janine saw that they were diaphanous, that she could almost see through them. How much more time was there? What could Janine do?

"I know what I feel Jannie, inside," Tia began,

"I know what's different. There is not so much more time."

"Don't say that, Tia," Janine said, "we've had so much more time than the doctors said. You don't know."

"No, I do, I know," Tia said, "and I have made some decisions. The first one is I want to live."

Janine felt her own face open and widen. Tia thought she was getting closer to death and it made her want to live. A panicky sadness filled Janine: she wanted her aunt to live, too; she wanted her to live forever and because Tia had not been afraid to die, Janine had come to believe she wouldn't. Tia said over and over again that she was ready to meet the Lord when He was ready for her but now she didn't want to go. Janine looked out the window but there was nothing to see in the sky but darkness. Was Jesus out there in the blackness now? If she stared hard enough, would she find out what to do?

"Tia, I want you to live, too," was all she could think of to say.

"Oh, no, dear, you don't understand what I want to say. I know my time is short now, I know because of what I feel. But with the time I have left, I want to live. I mean really live, like the way I lived before I got so sick. I want to get out of this bed and come into the kitchen. I want to sit in the wheelchair there so I can help you cook. I want to eat meat and drink coffee and maybe a glass of wine, play cards, listen to music, go for a walk around the block. I don't want to sleep in the daylight anymore."

"But Tia, you get so tired."

"I will have plenty of time to sleep when I am with the Lord," she said. "But now, during the days I have left, I want to be alive. I want to teach you how to roast a leg of lamb. You will go get some new magazines and read them to me. We can rent movies. I'll sleep at night like normal people, except on Sundays. On Sundays, I will take a nap while you are at church."

"Oh, Tia, I don't think I can go to church...it's been so long and I..."

"You'll go. I've discussed it with the Father. It's settled. He's expecting you on Sunday."

Janine nodded her head.

* * *

By 1:00 the chicken soup was ready and when Janine brought it to her aunt, Tia was propped up watching "Days of Our Lives."

"Marlena, you ARE the Salem stalker, I knew it," Tia said to an attractive blonde woman on the television screen, the one who Tia had claimed was often possessed by the devil. Janine set the tray with the soup down on Tia's lap and gave her the spoon. Tia was transfixed to the screen and took a spoonful of the soup without looking at it. Then she stopped.

"This is your soup?" Tia asked, taking another spoonful and then another.

"Of course. I've been making you soup for weeks and weeks."

"Not like this you haven't," she said.

"I guess it was the gizzards and innards."

"The gizzards and innards?"

Janine told Tia about Harris, the butcher, about

how for this soup he picked out a better chicken than the one she had picked out herself, and how he had told her to use everything to make the soup.

Tia finished her soup and asked for a second bowl.

"Leave it to a butcher," Tia said, "this soup will save me." Perhaps it was Janine's imagination or wishful thinking, but the warm rich soup had given Tia a pink glow that she hadn't had since Janine had started cooking for her.

"A butcher knows," Tia said, putting her finger to her temple. "And you see? I told you. It's better to go to the store at night. So this butcher," and now her eyes seemed to be twinkling, "he's your age? A nice boy? Someone you like?"

"He's a man, Tia," Janine said and heard herself saying it with a nervous laugh, "he's as old as Daddy."

"Is he married? Is he handsome? And what religion? He's a Catholic?"

"Tia," Janine tried again, "he's the butcher at the grocery store. I don't know anything about him. He's Daddy's age. He's just the butcher; he helps me find the meat." She was not going to tell Tia about the tulip.

"You'll get your hair cut this weekend, Janine."
* * *

Sometimes when Janine got to the store in the middle of the night, Harris was not there. At first, his absence made her feel more relaxed but then she also knew that when her eyes flicked up and around the store, she was looking for him. She told herself it was for protection: she needed to be ready in case he assaulted her again with compliments and paper flowers. Yet Tia had definitely improved since Harris had taken it upon himself to supervise all of Janine's meat buying; he also often appeared in other aisles she was in and insisted she buy his favorite brands. He would say things like, "You are buying the juice? Buy the Goya. It is sweet and thick and delicious. You will like it. You are a juicy girl" or, "No, no, don't buy that peach. Here, buy this, papaya. It is young and ripe...you know about these kind of fruit," and then he would laugh and wink at her as if he had made a joke she understood. And she would smile back because she wanted to understand. Harris' English was imperfect and so there were many times when Janine couldn't comprehend what he was saying, or what he meant, yet she didn't want to embarrass him and she was as afraid to ask him as she was to raise her hand in high school. Sometimes her instincts told her that he was saying something to her that she should not be hearing and then she felt herself getting clammy and nervous: but the things he told her to buy were universally superior to the things she had come into the store to get and Tia, in her pleasure at the new tastes and smells, seemed to have forgotten about sending Janine to church.

"This butcher, this Harris," Tia would say, swallowing a fragrant spoonful of mashed sweet plantains Harris had convinced her to buy and then told her how to make, "he is a good man. A smart man. I live for this food."

Often the boss Gonzalez would be wandering around the store and seeing Janine there every night, he had come to know her and to say hello. He would also say something to Harris every time like "only helping out the customer, Harris?" or when he found them in another aisle, "they need you in the meat department, Harris" and Harris would always reply with something that didn't make complete sense, such as "no problems here, boss" or "nothing to worry about here, boss, I know, I know." Again, Janine could feel something not quite right in these exchanges but she chalked it up to her own inability to understand the meaning inside his broken phrases. Yet Gonzalez's English was the same as her own and he seemed to understand Harris perfectly.

One Friday, Janine shopped in the middle of the night for the entire weekend because that afternoon, Father MacMahon had asked why he hadn't seen Janine at the coffees after Sunday mass and suddenly Tia remembered church and insisted Janine have a full night's sleep before the mass on Sunday. Although she had won the battle about the haircut, Janine had let Tia put a bit of blush and lipstick on her face to test it out; and she had reluctantly agreed to wear a pink and yellow flowered dress that Tia had remembered Janine having in high school.

"Don't you think these colors are little much for church?" Janine had asked.

"It's church, not a funeral," Tia had answered.

"Right...but it's church, not a dating service," Janine had countered. She knew what her aunt and the priest were up to.

"Ok, but after the mass, it's a church social. Now show me what shoes you plan to wear."

Harris found Janine in the canned goods aisle on

Friday night and asked her why her cart was so full.

"And look at what you have? Baby food? You have the baby?" He looked genuinely shocked.

"No, no baby," Janine said, and then she told Harris about Tia.

Harris listened intently as Janine briefly explained Tia's condition, the uncertainty, her aunt's love of meat and difficulty eating almost anything that wasn't soft. She told him how many of the things he had already suggested to her were making her aunt very happy. The next thing Janine knew, Harris was wheeling her cart up and down the aisles, putting items in it that she had no idea what she would do with. When they got to the meat department, he said, "wait here. I come back for you in ten minutes. Don't leave."

Without knowing it, Harris had already contributed so much to Tia's will to live that Janine waited; plus, she needed an explanation of all the items he'd put in her cart. When he came back out, it was with five index cards on which he written recipes for things with meat that she could cook that her Tia would be able to eat. Janine looked at the scratchy handwriting and broken directions and raised her eyebrows.

"So easy," he said, "delicioso. Your Tia, she love them. Good for her, too. Cornmeal and the black beans," he said holding up one card and pointing to items he'd put in her cart, "and this meat you cook for long time," holding up another. "Everything else, you cook fast. So good for you, too. You cook fast and then go out."

Janine didn't know if she would be able to

decipher the recipes let alone make the foods but she was so touched by the gesture that she said, "Thank you so much, Harris." It was the first time she had called him by his name.

"So, what? You got a nurse when you go out?"

"No, I don't need to. Tia sleeps while I'm here at the store."

"But what about out?" Harris asked, "the clubs. What you do you when you go to the clubs? Who watches your Tia then?"

"I don't go to clubs," Janine said, in a voice that made it sound as though it was the most obvious thing in the world.

"No clubs? So what then? The bars, the hotels? What you do for your Tia when you must go out?"

"I don't go out," Janine said, a fact of her life yet saying it to Harris at that moment made it seem as preposterous as the idea of Janine going out.

"A woman like you," Harris said with a sigh but also with an odd smile, "need more. You should need to go out, dancing, the salsa, some music. To go out. Get education."

"To school?" Janine asked, not knowing how he went from the salsa to education but ready to tell him she had finished school.

"Ah, I teach you," he said, with the wink Janine was used to by now. "I take you to the school."

"I graduated from high school," Janine said, but Harris only looked at her.

"You need to go to the high place," he finally said.

"I'm going to church on Sunday."

"Ayiee," Harris responded, "so, what? You have a

date with Jesus?"

"Something like that," Janine replied.

The more Janine got to know Harris, the less she compared him to her father although there were some similarities: Harris looked out for her in the grocery store the way her father had tried to look out for her at home and in the world. When her father could not protect her, could not get up off the floor after the robbers had beat him bloody, he cried when she visited him in the hospital and after he was released, he went away. But Harris was always at the store when Janine was there. Once, when some drunken teenagers smashed their cart into hers, Harris appeared and told them to get lost. Another time, she was reaching for a package of ground meat just as a man was reaching for the same package and when she stepped back to let him take it, he began yelling at her. Again, Harris appeared and calmed the man down, made him apologize to Janine and then walked her to the van to be sure she would be safe.

After the paper tulip, Harris gave her little things sometimes, the way her father had: once a little notebook to keep recipes in, once two jars of salsa he said he made and put in the blender for Tia to have on her mashed beans. But Harris was funnier than her father had been, and not as serious; Janine thought he must have a better life, a nice wife who liked his cooking, some children who were happy and good.

The other difference was that Harris treated Janine like a grown-up instead of like a child; Janine felt the difference but thought it was because she was not his child, and not because she was a woman. No

one had ever seen to it that Janine would come to
an understanding of what belonged to growing up.
From the time her parents left, she remained virtually
the same except that she understood how life could
change from habit to horror in a split second when
the robbers, with ski masks over their heads, held
her wrists behind her back and shoved her into her
apartment. She learned some other things about
change then, too. She saw her mother's fury fade
and her father's kindness turn to bewilderment when
they beat him and took the few valuable things the
family owned. She watched her parents change before
her eyes and then disappear. But although Janine
had aged, she had not gotten any older: fear froze
in permanent plates within her and then freed her in
the most unlikely way by keeping her to the smallest
possible universe, the one she knew and could inhabit
and control. She thought that she knew the worst
things about the world, that she had lived through
them. But in the last few weeks, surprised by her
ability to go places and do things she could never have
imagined, the plates began to thaw and shift inside
Janine.

On Saturday morning, she was at the stove
making ropa vieja, a Cuban recipe of shredded beef
and vegetables that Harris had given her. It was his
mother's recipe and the directions showed Janine how
to cook it so that the pieces of meat would be small
and tender enough for Tia to swallow.

Tia was in the kitchen in her wheelchair, nodding
and smiling in anticipation at the smells coming off
the stove.

"Your friend Mr. Harris, he must be a fine cook," Tia said. "One day you will put me in the van and we will go to the store so I can meet him and thank him. What did you say? He is around 30? Not married?"

"No, Tia, I said I don't know how old he is, around Daddy's age...and I'm sure he's married. So stop trying to fix me up with the butcher, ok? It's bad enough that I have to go to church."

"Church? Church is for you and God. I don't know what you're talking about."

"Well, God doesn't care if I wear a flowered dress and lipstick but you seem to...I know what you and Father Mac are up too."

"Nonsense," Tia said, tsking. "But you're not getting any younger, you know...and I won't be around forever."

"Yes you will," Janine said, laughing. She was not used to laughing and it struck her at that moment that she was genuinely happy. Just then, the phone rang.

"It's August already, Janine, Jesus Christ."

"Jesus rocks," Janine said back into the phone. It was her mother.

"What? What did you say?" Her mother's voice was still sharp and grating, the way it had always been.

"Nothing, Mother. How are you?"

When Tia heard Janine say "Mother" she rolled her eyes and shook her head.

"How am I? Well, let's see. I haven't heard from you or your aunt in weeks. I don't even know if she's dead or alive."

"She's mighty alive," Janine said. Janine had

never spoken to her mother like that before. Then she winked at Tia.

"Hello Loretta," Tia called out.

"Hear that, Mother?" Janine said. "Tia's here in the kitchen with me. We're cooking."

"Don't give me 'you're cooking'—what's going on over there?"

Janine couldn't explain what was going on and only knew that she wanted it to keep going on forever. She and Tia had become more like girlfriends than a shy niece taking care of a dying great aunt and Janine was having fun for the first time in her life so she said "Everything's fine here" and when her mother snorted at that answer, Janine changed the subject by asking, "How's Ornelle?"

Ornelle was the man Janine's mother met her second month in Atlanta. He worked with Loretta's sister. They lived in a trailer on the outskirts of the city.

"Ornelle is fine. What is your plan, Janine? It's August."

"Yes..." Janine said.

"Well, have you forgotten that you have a job? Who will stay with Tia then, when you go back to work?"

Janine had not thought about that. She had forgotten about her own life. "I don't know, Mother. I'll figure something out."

When Janine's mother had left for Atlanta, she took three suitcases filled with all of her own clothes and the ones of Janine's that she had convinced herself looked good on her. "Your aunt's apartment is paid for, she has money. She'll buy you clothes," Loretta

had said when Tia and Janine drove her to the bus
station in the big gray van. "Sell your father's damn
car if you need to," she said. "I'll call you when I get
there." Since then, Janine and Tia hardly ever heard
from Loretta and when they did, it was never to
inquire about their health or their plans. Now her
concern that Janine figure out what to do when school
started again was disarming.

"Well, you'd better figure it out soon," her mother
said, "I can't believe she's still alive."

"Tia's fine," Janine insisted. "She's not ready to
meet Jesus."

Tia laughed but Loretta said, "For Christ's sake,
Janine, What is the matter with you?' and Janine said,
"Mother, please don't use the Lords' name in vain."

"Oh, I can see your aunt has been a great
influence on you. What about the future, Janine?
What the hell do you plan to do with your future? Do
I have to come there? I don't have time to come there,
Janine."

"You don't need to come here, Mother. Everything
is fine. I'll think about what to do when school opens
and then I'll call you. I have to go now. Bye," and she
hung up the phone, something she had never done
before. She looked at Tia with real surprise and Tia
nodded her head in approval. When Loretta called, it
was because she needed something—her stereo, which
Janine packed up and shipped to Atlanta, a winter
coat she had in the back of her closet, a box of old
books she'd bought at a garage sale that she thought
were worth something but turned out not to be. The
last call Janine had before Tia got sick was full of

Loretta's complaining about money. She knew Tia
had some.

If Loretta was calling now, it had to be because
she thought Tia was dying and that some of that
money was due her.

* * *

On Sunday morning, Janine put on the dress, the
lipstick and a pair of sandals; Tia had insisted she
polish her toenails.

"You are a picture," Tia said, "now go wow
them."

"Tia, I'm going to church."

"Linger at the coffee social, dear. Don't worry
about me; I'll be fine."

"Well, the phone's right there and I have the cell
phone so call me if you need anything, ok?"

"Go, Tia said. "Go to God."

"It's 'go with God' Tia."

"He knows."

The church was so crowded that Janine almost
turned back; she had never liked being around a lot
of people and that feeling had grown stronger over
the last few weeks, especially since she had taken to
going to the near-empty grocery store in the middle
of the night. But she had promised Tia and Father
MacMahon that she would go to church so she ended
up squeezing into the end of a pew beside a family
of eight, the parents and their six children. Two were
teenagers and the rest were under ten years old but
they were miraculously well-behaved throughout the
mass.

Father MacMahon's voice roamed in her head

but she really did not hear what he was saying. She was thinking about the phone call from her mother. What *would* she do in a couple of weeks when school started and she was expected back at work? The job in the Kindergarten classroom was easy and as long as Janine remained hyper-vigilant and did what was expected of her, no one criticized or ridiculed her, yelled at her or rolled their eyes. But she had never really been happy there: she knew this because she felt happy now. All her life, Janine knew what it felt like to be unhappy, to be frustrated, powerless, frightened, unsure but then on the weekends how it felt to be safe and content because her father would be home and her mother would go out. After the robbery, Janine thought she knew what it felt like to be a trapped bird, to be a small body with panicked wings flying around a house of noise banging and bruising herself against windows that were locked tight. After her father left, she knew what it felt like to be inconsolable and when her mother left, she discovered what it felt like to be relieved. Since she had been living with Tia, all of those feelings had congealed and separated into rooms inside her and her reliance on keeping those rooms small and neat let her make a kind of safe house within herself: at work and other places she had to go in the world, her fear rose and surrounded her and that was like a small house too, one that shaped everything she did but gave her an ironic safety: she would never be taken by surprise by anything again. Once back at Tia's, she climbed the stairs of relief and her breath came easier but never slow enough to lose what she would need if the unexpected threatened her again. Until Tia got sick, she believed that living was nothing more than location and relocation, moving between the house of fear and the house of calm but then she found her true home: taking care of Tia and all that came with that—cooking, shopping at night, her unlikely friendship with Harris, reading aloud, listening to music, rubbing her aunt's feet until they were warm and pink—made her happy.

She looked at the family sitting next to her in church and knew that although she was supposed to want what she had grown up learning that girls want—to get married, have children, make a family— she was as happy as they were.

Janine did not know if such a revelation would have come to her anywhere else besides church, and she looked up at the carved ceiling and thanked Jesus through the open skylight. She felt peaceful and thought that maybe, when it was time, she would like to meet him. For the first time in her life, she understood what her aunt felt when she prayed, when she so easily put her faith into God's hands. The Father's voice was gently receding out of her head and being replaced with something Janine could not remember ever having thought about—making plans. Suddenly, she found herself deciding that she would talk more to Harris about cooking, about different kinds of dishes and ways to prepare them. She would bypass the library and go to a bookstore and buy some cookbooks she could own and write in, full of recipes she could explore, memorize. She would quit her job and take the best care of Tia that she could. When she got home, she would call her mother to tell her that she had a future.

But first, Janine would keep her promise and
attend the coffee social. The hall was packed with
parishioners sipping drinks out of Styrofoam cups,
nibbling on store-bought cookies and seemingly
catching up with neighbors and friends. At first, Janine
thought that her anxiety reappeared because she did
not know where to put herself. She saw a group of
people her own age clustered at the end of the cookie
table but she didn't know them and thought she
did not know how to join them; but then she knew
something that was absolutely sure: she did not want
to join them. She simply was not interested. Her
anxiety was impatience: she wanted to go home.

She looked around for Father MacMahon in the
crowd and finally saw him at the opposite end of
the big square room. She could make her way over
there, just to say hello, to show him she had come, to
thank him for the sermon she didn't actually hear but
that had framed her thinking; she could thank him
for the way his urging and his voice had given form
to years of amorphous thoughts and feelings that
she had never known what to do with. But, instead,
Janine ate a cookie, drank half a cup of tepid coffee
and went home. She may not have had the experience
Father MacMahon wanted her to have, but she had
been transported all the same. When he came by the
apartment to see Tia, she knew she would be able to
make him understand.

When she first got back to the apartment, she
thought she heard the television but by the time she
got into Tia's room, she knew with dark certainty that

it wasn't even turned on.

"You need to be realistic, Tia," her mother was saying.

"About what?" Tia asked, "that I'm going to die? I think I know that, Loretta."

"Mother," Janine said, walking into the room, her face flush with anger. "What are you doing here?"

Loretta looked at her daughter in disbelief; of course Janine had never spoken to her mother like that before. But all these years that Janine had spent protecting herself and now her aunt, of sleeping with a baseball bat at her side, of wondering what she would do if threatened again, settled her fear into power. Janine had had her home invaded once before and had lost something precious. She was not about to let it happen again.

"What are you doing here, Mother?" Janine repeated.

"Well, I couldn't get a straight answer out of you. So I drove all night to get here. So what? You're going to church now?"

"Just this once," Janine said.

"How was it?" Tia asked.

"Remarkable," Janine said, a word she realized had never come out of her mouth before. Tia smiled triumphantly.

"Sit down, Janine. I don't have a lot of time."

"Oh, that's funny," Tia said. Janine looked up and smiled.

"I came here because I don't know what the hell is going on with you two. Your aunt is sick and you are taking care of her. Fine. But your job is going to

start up again in a couple of weeks and I would like
to know what kind of plans you have. I have a right
to..."

"You gave up your rights, Loretta, when you left."
Tia said.

"Tia," Loretta said in a false heavy voice, as if
she was talking to a child she did not like, "you don't
understand. Let me talk to Janine."

"I understand perfectly well. I have cancer, not
dementia. I know exactly why you're here. You want
money: it's the only thing that would get you into a
car and drive all night. It's the only thing that would
get you here. But you've come to the wrong place,
dearie."

"I didn't come here for your money, Tia."

"Then for what, Loretta?"

"I came here because I was worried..."

"About what?" Tia snapped. "About me? About
my health? Were you worried about your daughter,
how she was doing, what she was doing?"

"Yeah, yeah, all of those things."

"Well, it's funny then, Loretta, because we haven't
heard from you in...when was the last time we heard
from your mother, Jannie?"

"May. When you were diagnosed, Tia."

"That's not true," Loretta said but you could tell
from the look on her face that she knew it was. Janine
had called her mother to say that Tia had cancer;
Loretta had said, "Fine. Call me when it's gets really
bad" and they had not heard from her until now.

"I'm sorry you came all the way here, Loretta.
There's nothing for you to do here. Or to have. I think

you should go."

"You may be my mother's sister, Tia, but you're not my mother. You don't tell me what to do."

"What do you know about being a mother?" Tia said.

"I know that I have a daughter here that owes me some answers and I'm not going anywhere until I get them." She turned to Janine: "I want to know your plans, Janine. If Tia dies," she said, as if Tia was not in the room, "are you going to sell this apartment? What will you do with that money? Where do you think you're going to go?"

"Why would she sell the apartment, Loretta," Tia said, "so you can get some money? This is her home." She was steadfast and it seemed as though the chance to finally say these things to Loretta was fortifying her.

But Janine had had enough. She and Tia hadn't seen Loretta since last Christmas, when her mother and Ornelle had come for one day under the auspice of the holiday but mostly to pick up the last few things Janine was storing for her mother. They brought Tia a tea set that had clearly been made for a six year old child's tea party and Janine, of all things, a stuffed doll. When Ornelle had given the gift to Janine, he looked confused as if he thought he was bringing a present to a much younger girl. They set the tea set on the kitchen table and placed the doll in one of the chairs. Then Ornelle set about making dinner. He had brought a frozen fried turkey that his cousin in Louisiana had mailed to him and that they then had driven to Miami from Atlanta but when they unwrapped it, it had clearly spoiled from all its travels.

It took days for the stench to leave the kitchen. They ate scrambled eggs and toast for Christmas dinner and early the next morning, Loretta and Ornelle were gone.

"You don't live her anymore, Mother, you don't have a say in what goes on."

"I'm gonna say what I came here to say. Tia needs to go into a home, you both know it. You have to go to work, Janine. And sell this apartment. I can't keep worrying about you."

"Worrying about her?" Tia said, "now that's a laugh."

"Well, I left her here with you, didn't I?" Loretta snapped.

"You left her," Tia said, and then she sighed, the fight in her having disappeared in resignation: there was no point in trying to reason with her niece.

"I'm not going into a home, Loretta," Tia said, "I am home. And you need to go back to your own home. But stay here for dinner with us first. Jannie is going to mash some potatoes and roast a pork loin."

"A pork loin? What kind of food is that for someone as sick as you?" Loretta said.

"I know. Your daughter is trying to kill me off," Tia said. Then she pulled the covers up to her neck and closed her eyes. Janine went to the kitchen.

"So since when do you know how to cook?" Loretta said, coming into the kitchen.

"I cook for Tia all the time." Janine turned the oven to 400, put a pot of water on the stove and began to peel the potatoes.

"You never cooked for me." Janine was going to

say you never cooked for me, either, but instead said, "Are you staying?"

"I don't exactly feel welcome."

Janine shook her head and sighed. There was a lot she could have said but none of it would have made any difference.

"You're welcome to stay for dinner," was what she chose.

"Well, you've turned into a regular snot," her mother said.

When Janine did not reply, her mother brought the apartment up again.

"Mother, did you see Tia? She is alive. She is wonderfully alive. She is not going into a home. We are not selling this apartment. If you need money now, I'll..."

"You'll sell your father's car then," Loretta said.

"No," Janine said, with force and without thought.

"Why not?"

"Because I need that car more than I need money," Janine said.

"What are you talking about? You've never driven that car. You drive Tia's van."

This was just one of many things Janine could never expect her mother to understand.

"Are you staying for dinner?" Janine asked her.

Loretta said no; it was a long drive back to Atlanta and she wanted to get started before it got dark.

"I'm sorry this trip didn't work out for you, Mother," Janine said. "I'm going to stay here as long as Tia needs me. I guess I'll give you a call when she doesn't anymore."

"You'd better tell me if you sell this apartment, young lady. Tia was my mother's sister: I'm owed some of that money. And speaking of money, don't even think about quitting your job."

"Actually, Mother, that's exactly what I'm thinking. I'm only twenty-two. I'll find another job."

"You don't know how to do anything."

"I do, Mother," Janine said, "I know how to take care of Tia."

* * *

On Monday morning, over coffee and corn meal mash, Tia decided she wanted spaghetti for dinner on Tuesday night; Janine would do her middle of the night shopping for the ingredients. "You can mash the sausage when it gets soft. Ask Harris. He'll know what kind goes good with the tomatoes. Get the little soft pastas. You'll wheel me into the kitchen. I'll show you."

Harris was standing in the front of the store when Janine walked in around 3:30 a.m.

"How was the weekend?" he asked her.

"More than I expected," she said.

"Oh, you have a date?" he asked.

"I went to church." She had no intention of telling Harris about her mother.

"So you have a date with Jesus?"

"Yeah, I wanted to meet him." Harris raised his eyebrows and while he followed Janine to produce, she told him about the Jesus fish on her car, how the woman on Alton Road had screamed at her, about the kids saying "Jesus rocks" in the parking lot. She heard herself talking and talking and had to stifle her own surprise. But Harris did not.

"Wow," he said, "I don't think you say so much to me since I meet you. I see now, I can understand."

But Janine did not. So she changed the subject.

"I have to make spaghetti tonight. With sausage. Tia wants you to pick it out," she said, embarrassed to have said so much and more so that Harris noticed.

"I know what you need," Harris said, with the wink. Janine had used it herself to forge a barrier with Tia against her mother: she understood complicity. "Go," he said, "get your vegetables. I meet you in meat. Ha, meet in meat. I am a comedian."

Janine started laughing, harder than Harris' joke warranted but laughing was freedom now. She picked out plum tomatoes with care, a large onion, some celery, a garlic. When she returned to the meat department, Harris had everything ready for Janine to make a delicious spaghetti: pork, sausage already ground fine, veal bones. He gave her a recipe card that explained how to prepare the bones and then steep them in the tomatoes.

"You make the hot sauce tonight, eh?" Harris said, pressing the package of meat and bones he had wrapped up for her into her torso. Although they knew each other so much better by now, Harris still made odd advances that still made Janine back away. She was getting used to Harris but she was not used to being touched.

"Yes, but not too hot. Tia can't have anything too hot."

"Can you?" he asked.

"I like hot food," she said.

"You are funny," Harris said, laughing.

"A comedian?" she asked.

"No, just funny. I never know you. You get it or you don't get it, I never know."

"I get it," Janine said because she wanted to understand, and she smiled because Harris was smiling and because smiling was easy and felt good.

"What's everyone smiling about?' Gonzalez had just come around the corner. "Everybody getting everything they need?"

"Sure thing, boss, Almost."

"Good. Good job, Harris. How are you doing tonight, Miss?"

"Fine, thanks," Janine said. Gonzalez was a nice man. He was serious and often looked tired but seemed as though he liked his job and was good at it. He watched over Harris. A good man.

"All right," Gonzalez said. "Take good care of the lady, Harris."

"Your bet, boss" Harris said, with the wrong word but a lot of enthusiasm, "I do that. I do that tonight, take good care of the lady."

Gonzalez nodded his head and walked away.

"Now he go to the office and sleep with the camera," Harris whispered.

"Sleep with the camera?"

"Yeah, the camera, the surveillance...in the aisles, the garage, the elevators, you know. He supposed to watch for crime but he sleep instead of that. You don't know this because you come too early...but tonight you are late, yes? Late and on the right time. Gonzalez nap time."

It was true. Janine had arrived about an hour later than usual; her mother's visit, although short, had worn her out and she had slept longer than she was used to. She looked at her watch; it was after 4:00.

"I need to go," she said with sudden urgency. "Sometimes Tia wakes up around 4:30. I need to be there when she gets up."

"Yeah, sure, we go, we go now," Harris said, and he put his hand in the small of her back to guide her toward the checkout.

We go now might have seemed an odd thing for Harris to say if Janine hadn't been so used to the way he tried to talk to her in English and not so consumed with the image of Tia waking up and calling out and Janine not being there. When they arrived at the check-out line, Harris did not leave and Janine did not notice until she heard the cashier say, "Harris, you're not a customer. Get out of the line." Her name was Ida and she was pointing her finger at Harris.

"I help with the customer," Harris said, "just like Gonzalez tell me."

"Oh, you'd better watch yourself," Ida said. "You know what happened last time." Ida was more serious than the other cashiers, at least it appeared that way.

"What happened last time?" Janine asked, suddenly aware that something was not right, partly because of Ida's comment but also because Harris still had his hand in the small of Janine's back.

"Nothing happens. I still here, yes?" He looked at Ida with a flat grin. "And Gonzalez, he don't watch me so much now. Now is the nap time."

Ida responded in Spanish and then Harris said something back to her. At first it seemed like joking but then they were volleying back and forth in rapid angry Spanish whispers. Janine felt the house of panic rise and it had been so long since she had felt nervous in the grocery store at night that the fear felt alien and uncomfortable. She thought something terrible was going to happen—their voices were getting louder and they started gesturing wildly at each other—but then just as quickly as they had gone from joking to anger, they were both laughing again. Janine was so relieved, she started to laugh too.

"You speak Spanish?" Ida said, whipping her head around to face Janine.

"No," Janine said.

"Then why are you laughing?" she asked.

But how could Janine explain? Simply by laughing, she had invaded a place, a privacy, where she didn't belong.

"I wouldn't be laughing if I were you," Ida said, and immediately looked down at her cash register keys. Janine felt her face and neck getting hot and red: she was humiliated and began to pack her own groceries very fast so she could leave. Harris and Ida were whispering now in Spanish and Janine began to hum some tuneless song in her head so she would not hear them. When her groceries were in her cart, she gave Ida $40.00 and started to walk away without her change.

"Your change," Ida said, and not nicely. Janine was so weak with embarrassment and the need to escape that when she reached out to get the change, the coins slipped through her palms onto the floor. She did not care. She stuffed the bills in her pants pocket and picked up her bags. She hadn't felt like this since the woman screamed at her on Alton Road weeks ago.

"Here, here, your money," Harris said, bending down to the floor to get her change. He also had one bag of her groceries that she had neglected to take.

"No, I don't care, leave it," she said, meaning the change but then seeing that Harris had the bag of groceries, "let's go."

"Ah, ok, you get it," Harris said. "See?" he said to Ida, "you wrong about this one" and he followed Janine out of the store.

Once through the doors, Janine reached out to take the bag from Harris but he shook his head no and smiled. He should be back in the meat department, not helping her with his groceries. He wasn't a bag boy. But the only other time Janine was upset in the grocery store, Harris had walked her to the van and clearly he could tell she was upset now. Maybe he was going to apologize for Ida's rude behavior. She was going to ask him but then didn't want to: she just wanted to get the groceries in the van and go home. She didn't understand how everything had gone wrong in two minutes in the grocery line. She didn't know how to get back to the place she knew when she was there.

On the escalator that went up to the parking garage she said, "I can take the bag, Harris," she said. "I have to go."

"We make the hot sauce for tonight,' Harris said.

Did he think he was coming home with her? That was ridiculous and made no sense and Janine knew that a lot of things Harris said made no sense but her normal empathy had been replaced by an annoyance she wasn't used to feeling. She just wanted to go home.

"I am making the hot sauce tonight, not for tonight," she said in an exasperated voice, correcting his English to his face. Obviously I don't know your language but you don't know mine either, she wanted to say but then realized her anger was the result of her humiliation. Ida had embarrassed her and embarrassment, unlike laughter, was a feeling Janine knew very well. After all these weeks of shopping at two o'clock in the morning, of meeting up with Harris every night, of saying hello to Gonzalez, chatting lightly with the cashiers, Janine had been relaxed and lured into believing she belonged, that she knew these people, that they were her friends.

But just because Janine had been humiliated didn't mean Harris deserved to be just because he mixed up his pronouns and put words in sentences where they didn't need to be. At least he had learned some English; what was her excuse? They reached the van and Harris helped her put the grocery bags in the back. Then she walked over to the driver's side door and opened it.

"I wish I knew Spanish," she said and was about to apologize for snapping and to thank him for all his help when he said, "I help you know the Spanish" and then his hands were on her waist and he was pressing himself up against her so hard that she was leaning backwards into the driver's seat.

"Get in," he whispered and his lips were at her neck. "Hurry" he said. He was still whispering but the sound was serious, almost mean, yet his voice was also conspiratorial. He misunderstood complicity and now, finally, when Janine understood it was too late.

"Go, go," he said more urgently now, before biting the skin on her neck and then her chin, "we don't have so much time" and then his open lips were on her own and he was kissing her and pushing her shoulders back and saying "Get in, get in the car. I know Gonzalez, he wake up sometime to look at the camera, go go."

When the shorter of the two robbers had pushed Janine down into a kitchen chair and tied her hands behind her back, he had taken one of his own hands and put it on her neck. She'd had on a button down shirt and that hand had started to move toward the V at the top of it when the other robber said, "not now, asshole. Check that cabinet. See if there's silver."

"I'm goin for gold," said the robber whose hand was moving on Janine's skin.

"You're gonna get this knife up your ass if you don't get away from that bitch and find the silver," the other robber said.

"Oh, Jesus," Loretta had said, "oh Jesus Christ, oh my Lord" and the robber had taken his hand away and gone to the cabinet. At the time, Janine thought her mother's outburst had been for her sake but then the robbers had taken the silver.

Harris had one hand on Janine's thigh and was

Jesus had shown her the light on Sunday. She had seen the light in the house of God.

"Oh Jesus," Janine said, running through the rooms that made up her life, looking for the one she had lived in at the hour in church but knocking down all the walls inside herself, all the structures that could have saved her.

"Oh yes, the Jesus," Harris said, his face so close to hers she could see the sweat pooling in his pores. "Yeah, you get it. Jesus, he rock. Jesus gonna rock you now. This your second date with Jesus."

When Janine closed her eyes, she was in one big room, like a waiting room, a room where you waited for the next thing to happen, for a car to come into the garage and want your space, for an ill Tia to wake up and call you, for your mother be sorry and your father to come home, for Gonzalez to feel your urgency and open even just one eye.

The Vendor

Salim was so relieved and excited when the hotel renegotiated its contract with the building company that he stayed up all night. He had seen the hotel people, in their suits and hard hats, shaking hands with Pete McCoy Sr. of McCoy Construction on the six o'clock news; behind them, the half completed hotel seemed to wobble in expectation. As soon as Salim heard they would resume work in the morning, he clapped his hands, got up from the couch, and went to work. He worked straight through the night and was not surprised to see that even after not sleeping, he felt fine.

Around five a.m., he began to dress. He pressed his white shirt carefully and he used a lot of steam. He pressed his beige trousers, too. They were old and out of style, the polyester kind with a wide rim and hook closure and slant pockets on each hip. Although they rarely wrinkled, Salim pressed them anyway.

He took his time showering; then, after shaving, he trimmed and combed his beard. Salim was short and dark with more than what seemed like a natural amount of hair. But he was neat and clean and trim. He cleaned his ears and then ran a file over his fingernails. He slicked his black hair back with a tonic and splashed on some cologne.

Salim selected a pair of beige sneakers that matched his trousers perfectly and he put them on now for the first time, with fresh white socks that had been dusted with talcolm powder. When he got home later that afternoon, his clothing would be covered with a fine film of sand and construction dust but it did not matter: Salim had many clean white shirts and as many pairs of beige polyester slacks. The shoes he would brush clean.

From his dresser top, he took two ballpoint pens and clipped them to the pocket of his shirt; he had yet to have an occasion to use either pen because no one ever asked him anything that couldn't be answered by pointing his finger but he liked to be prepared. Then he put a roll of bills of varying denominations in his pants pocket. Looking in the mirror, Salim felt happy and nervous, the way a man feels when he is about to go on a job interview or a first date.

The truck had been packed and ready to go since four; he was prepared for two shifts. Looking at the clock on the kitchen wall, Salim knew he had ten minutes to spare so he poured a tall glass of cold water from the tap and sat down at his small kitchen table. He sipped his water and fingered the two apples sitting in the small bowl. His cousin in Cleveland had sent him a gift basket of food for his birthday; it had arrived almost two weeks ago and the apples were all that remained. Salim had been very careful about eating the delicacies the basket contained: a bit of sausage with some cheese on a cracker for breakfast, a chocolate-covered biscuit with some coffee at lunch; for dinner, Salim cooked a small amount of the fancy pasta and tossed it with the dark green olive oil that had come in a small bottle. Before bed, he would have an orange or a handful of grapes or almonds. In this way, he made the basket last a long time and savored every item in it. It was good of his cousin to remember him. During the hotel's hiatus, when all work had abruptly stopped and the newscasters kept reporting that no one knew when it would resume, Salim had toyed with the idea of driving up to Cleveland to visit his cousin, from whom he learned his trade. He would drive the truck up and Habib would be surprised and proud of how well Salim was doing. But then the hotel reached an agreement with Pete McCoy.

Once Salim had finished his water, used the bathroom and brushed his teeth, he decided to leave. He would drive slowly, as he normally did, and look carefully at things as he made his way to Miami Beach.

Salim drove down McDonald Street, admiring the heavy palm and poinciana trees, the lush hibiscus and other flowering bushes whose names he did not know. Although he had lived in Miami for the last twenty of his forty-two years, he still felt like a visitor sometimes. This, he believed, was partly because he did not know the names of all the flora indigenous to the area; to compensate, he made names up: rhodotilia, copercini, balboa. Salim liked the way the names sounded in his head, the

ways the invented names of plants and bushes came
to define them. He never got tired of the beauty,
never became complacent about seeing a fiery red
bloom or a bush full of fat soft pink flowers. In
front of the apartment building where Salim lived,
there were two flowering plants and two small trees
that bore tiny white blooms; every morning, Salim
plucked one petal away and touched it to his cheek.
Cellucia, Salim would think, Good Morning little
flower.

The house at the corner of McDonald had
early risers. Lights were on and Salim imagined
the elderly couple who lived there were having
some tea and putting on their tennis shoes, getting
ready for the morning walk that started their day.
When Salim was out of work, he spent a lot of
time driving down the familiar and the new streets,
wondering who lived in the houses he passed and
trying to imagine the different lives. On the streets
that neatly bordered his apartment building, he
actually knew a lot about his neighbors. Farther
down on McDonald lived a librarian and her
accountant-husband; Salim had a library card
and even though the library was supposed to be a
quiet place, the librarian liked to talk to her sister
on the phone during slow hours. She married
late, in her forties, and had decided not to have
children; instead, she and her husband spent what
extra money they saved on re-doing their kitchen,
building a stone patio and a small Japanese garden
with a pond and some exotic fish in their backyard.
Every other year, they went on a big vacation:

Seattle, Las Vegas, last year Montreal.

In the large pink house behind Salim's building lived the Masons: the mother, tall and blonde and sleek, was a real estate agent whose advertisements were in the newspaper and on the television all the time; her husband was a doctor who every year spent two weeks in Haiti caring for the poor, so he was on the television, too; they had two teenage children, a girl who played tennis at the park down the street and who was tutored in math by a teacher who lived on Salim's floor and a boy a year older who was a computer whiz. Once, when Salim had ventured into a computer store thinking he might want to email his cousin, the boy was there and he was explaining an operating system to one of the clerks. On the weekends, Dr. Mason grilled fish with a marinade made from imported oils and herbs from his wife's windowsill herb garden. Salim could see it all from his bedroom window.

Salim came to a stop sign and to a full stop. To his right he spotted a woman in a green BMW. She looked to be in her fifties, with a blonde helmet-like hairdo, pursed lips, bloated cheeks and overly made-up eyes. She probably drank, Salim thought. He trusted his instincts: his work was an education in knowing people. He smiled at her because he was sorry for her and then motioned that she could go first. The woman just rolled her eyes at him and accelerated through the intersection. As he slowly pulled away, Salim knew this woman could not live in his neighborhood.

Three blocks down, at the turn onto Main

Highway, was a private school; it was summer
but on the school fence were clusters of brightly
colored balloons. Summer camp, Salim thought,
satisfied with his deduction. He imagined the range
of children inside: little ones with matching play
outfits, tired bored adolescents in shorts and t-shirts
chasing them around. For lunch there would be hot
dogs or sloppy joes or macaroni and cheese. Salim
turned right after the school and headed toward the
interstate.

Driving his truck down I-95 took more than
the usual care he took with driving. In Miami,
there were so many people, too many who learned
to drive in places where there were few rules, who
caused a great amount of anxiety on the roads.
But Salim had the additional problem of having
to be very careful of his truck: things could not
be jostled. He merged carefully and smoothly into
the lane he needed and drove just under the speed
limit. Periodically, he would allow himself a split-
second glance at the cars passing him in the next
lane. The fast ones, he knew, lived in Miami and
were on their way to work; those who drove more
tentatively were tourists, unsure of which exit to
take, unwilling to end up in a bad neighborhood,
Miami having a dangerous reputation for tourists.
Salim wanted to reassure these people so he would
tap his horn a couple of times and wave as slower
drivers went by. On the side of his truck in thick
bold letters read SALIM: Hello, he would think
from within the truck cab. Welcome to Miami.

Salim took Exit 2D, the MacArthur Causeway,

and headed toward Miami Beach. On the left were
huge elaborate mansions; on the right, the Port
of Miami and the massive cruise ships readying
themselves to leave. On both sides so much money.
Expensive clothing, lush food, leather shoes and
furs and extravagant small items like earrings, tie
clasps, alligator wallets, fountain pens. Certainly
people in the mansions were waking slowly, lazily.
After coffee on the terrace, they would dress for
a day at the spa, the fancy mall, a meeting of
some board or other, lunch at Azul. On the ships,
workers were cleaning rooms, steaming lobsters,
straightening blouses in the shops, counting chips
in the casinos. Salim could see the hundreds of
passengers lined up on the decks, waiting for the
ship to pull out of port.

  As Salim drove, he liked to think about the
number of people in the world—even in the little
worlds that existed on either side of his truck as
it drove the speed limit down the causeway—and
how each one's individual life and job and necessity
meant something very large in and of itself. He
thought about all of the people on the ship and
how they had all come from somewhere, from
little towns or big cities, from farms or high rise
buildings. To prepare, they would have washed
and packed their summer clothes, their fun clothes,
remembering hats and sunglasses and, at the last
minute, journals they ended up never writing in.
They had saved for a year for this one week on
the ocean, for people to turn their beds down and
bring them fancy drinks. They would take pictures

of the natives on the islands they visited and of
each other in various places on the big ship: there
might even be a picture with the ship's captain in
his white uniform with gold bars on the shoulders.
They would take pictures of the food they were
served: lobsters, mountains of fresh shrimp, tropical
fruit salads, seven-layer chocolate and coconut
cakes. But the week would go by too quickly and
before they knew it, they would be home again.
They would be pulling into their driveways, five
pounds fatter and peeling from sunburn, and
while the children unpacked, the parents would be
sorting the mail that had piled up and watering the
lawns that had overgrown, making grocery lists,
doing laundry. The mother would swear she was
only going to eat salad for the rest of the summer
and the father would scratch his head and wonder
how long it would take to pay for the week that
was over; the children, no matter what age, would
lament the absence of waiters, busboys and maids,
the end of sneaking into bars and downing drinks
while their parents were dancing to big band music
and forgetting who they were. Each individual life
would resume itself all over again. Salim sighed
with the relief of his safe return to routine. He
did not understand the concept of vacation: he
did not understand something so hard earned
being so ephemeral and leaving one so full of
disappointment, fear and despair.

Bon Voyage, he said to the cruise ships as his
truck neared the end of the causeway, at least have
a Bon Voyage.

At the light at the end of the causeway was the terminal for Fisher Island, one of the most posh and expensive places to live in the United States. One could not just go to Fisher Island: the only way to get there was to put your car on a ferry and your name had to be on the Ferry Master's list. Salim had had his name on that list once for two straight months. He had taken the truck over there on the ferry when new construction was being done on the clubhouse. Every day he was there, he marveled at the idea that there was a private island where one could live. The condominiums were classy and lush but they all looked exactly the same and the people looked exactly the same, too: the white, skinny women with tight tan faces, the rosy children, the important men wearing casual clothes and talking on cell phones. Salim saw them all. And they saw him as they rode past the construction site in golf carts on their way to the golf course, the restaurant, the spa or the beach. Fisher Island residents had a beach where attendants knew everyone's name and set each person up with a chair, two soft folded white towels, and a little table for food or drinks. Each resident was greeted by name and given whatever they wanted. Salim thought it would be a miracle to live in such a place, and he felt sorry for the cruise goers.

The light for cars coming off the Fisher Island ferry turned green and the parade of Jaguars and Mercedes and even a Bently or two began. Someone honked. Hello, hello, thought Salim, to whoever it was who had obviously recognized him from the old clubhouse job. Once again, he was assured that painting SALIM in big letters on the side of his truck had been a fine idea.

Now his light changed and he traversed the bridge to South Beach. He drove down Fifth Street to Collins Avenue. Certainly there were other, quicker, ways to go but Salim liked to drive through the heart of South Beach. Tourists. Models. Movie stars. Once he had seen Gloria and Emilio Estefan, once Nikki Taylor and once a famous rap star he had seen on TV but whose name he did not know. Once he was very sure he saw Clint Eastwood look at his truck and smile. Was it a nostalgic smile? Had Mr. Eastwood been near a job where Salim might have been? It was possible: Salim had been everywhere in Miami and Miami Beach with his truck. But only during the day. Salim did not go out at night. When he was working, he had to cook all night; otherwise, nothing would get done. And when he was not working, he had neither the money nor the interest to go out: restaurants were overpriced, clubs were dangerous. Salim would not know what to do if he didn't have enough money to pay for a restaurant bill or if he got in trouble in a big crowded club and in those dark places, no one would be able to read in his face that he needed help.

Salim pulled into the half-constructed hotel at the corner of Collins and Lincoln Road. He had missed this building and the childhood memory that it inspired of his old broken house, the parts of walls that were left blackened by fire. There had

been shards of glass everywhere on the ground,
even beneath Salim as he laid curled up on the
cement, his own blanket wrapped around his
throat. It wasn't a good memory but it was all he
had left. And there wasn't much left of it except
his having been put to bed wrapped in that same
blanket only moments before. A severe pain had
flamed in his chest and he thought he had tried to
stand up and go to the building, go and get what
was his inside. But then Habib's mother came and
carried him away. Was he three or four then? He
did not remember.

But this broken building was the hotel and
looking at it, Salim felt comfort because he knew
it would take an endless amount of time to finish.
Although they had put in the palm trees and the
fountain and laid bricks in an intricate pattern
along the entrance, only half the building was
completed on the outside and less within. The
last time Salim had been to the hotel, nearly four
months ago, he had arrived to find a completely
abandoned work site. Salim had gotten out of the
truck and walked around, looking for someone. He
went inside and saw that the halls were constructed
and rooms had been cut out but nothing else
had been done. No wires or plumbing or paint
or carpet. Bare light bulbs hung from the ceiling
but they were turned off. It was dark and eerie as
Salim made his way through the hallways and then
up a set of temporary stairs. He was just about to
descend when he heard a voice shouting at him.

"What are you doing here?" a security guard in

a blue uniform wanted to know.

I work here, Salim thought, shrugging his shoulders as if the guard should already know.

"You don't know?" the guard said. "Well, I know you're not supposed to be here. The company's pulled out and ain't no one supposed to be here now. Come on," and he motioned for Salim to follow him down the stairs.

Now across the way Salim saw Juan and Frank and Jose and Jorge: they were not smiling because already, even at 7:30 in the morning, it was very hot and humid. There was a whole day of hard work ahead of them and they were not happy. But Salim was overjoyed, knowing how much work remained to be done.

He got out of the truck and went around to the side of the cab. There was his name—SALIM—no one could miss that. But most of them knew it anyway. He lifted the side of the truck wall up and pulled down the awning, which also displayed his name. Juan looked up when he heard the noise.

Juan was talking to Pete McCoy Sr. and his son, Pete Jr. who wanted to go to college, to the University of Miami, and so he was working for his father to pay his own way. He talked about it all the time while Salim heated up a turkey and cheese sandwich for his lunch, plain on white bread. Sometimes he liked potato chips, too.

Encino Benito's rowdy crew pulled up in the open pick-up truck. Encino's wife had some skin cancer last time I was here, Salim remembered. I hope she is better. As the workmen piled out of the

truck, Salim recognized many of the old boys—
Enrique, Eduardo, Anthony and Ricky. There were
a few new ones too. No matter, Salim thought, I
will know them soon enough.

"What're those?" Juan came up pointing,
"donuts?"

Salim had made the cruellers himself. They were
like donuts, but lighter. With honey.

"Those curly things? I'll have four of 'em. And
two coffees," Juan said.

He will like them better than donuts, Salim
knew and he handed Juan his order.

"Gracias," Juan said as he walked away.

The two Petes came up and Salim already had
Junior's English Muffin with egg and cheese in the
microwave; Pete Senior's ham croquette he was
wrapping in waxed paper. He handed Senior the
croquette and poured two coffees, one with cream
and one with milk.

"Ha," Pete Senior said, "how'd you know that?
You the guy who was here before?"

Pete Senior had a funny sense of humor. Salim
gave him his breakfast and knew it would fortify
him so he could do good work.

Four Benitos workers came up and one asked,
"Is there lunch yet?"

Of course. There was always lunch, breakfast
and lunch. Salim was always ready for shift one
and shift two.

"Whatdaya have?" one asked, this one with a
thin greasy mustache and unwashed hair. He must
be new, Salim thought, as everyone knew what

Salim had in his truck. Lamb kebobs. Eggplant
Parmesan. Chicken casserole. Rigatoni with meat.
Cheeseburgers, turkey burgers, chicken sandwiches
and grilled cheese. Tuna salad, egg salad, roast
beef rolled with cheddar cheese, tomatoes stuffed
with tabouleh. Hummus with cucumbers in pita,
cold tortellinis with broccoli and carrots. Green
salad, Cesar salad, chicken salad (with grapes), and
a new salad with couscous, raisins and almonds.
Foccacia pizzas with artichokes and olives. Philly
Cheesesteak.

"Jeez," a Benito worker said, "Jeez" as he
looked at the choices.

"Do you have soup?" another guy asked. "I
have a cold."

Soup? Chicken, vegetable barely, cream of
mushroom, gazpacho.

"Gimme chicken soup and one of those rolls,
ok?"

The soup was steaming hot and Salim waved
the cup in the air for a second to cool it a bit so the
man with the cold wouldn't burn his mouth.

"Good soup," the Benito guy said sipping
from the styrofoam cup. "Good and hot." Salim
didn't know his name but he would find out: all
day they called out to each other; all day they said
each other's names. Sometimes they would joke
around while they worked and Salim found them
very funny. Other times they would call out to each
other for things they needed: a hammer, the clip-
board, something to measure the windows with.
Cell phones would ring and owners would answer,

"This is Jose" or "Alex here" and if the calls were
work related, Salim would learn more about the
hotel's problems and progress. When the calls were
personal, Salim got to know the workers better. A
young one, Arturo, had a wife who was pregnant;
she called all the time and complained of being
sick. Perhaps Arturo would bring her home some of
Salim's chicken soup: very soothing.

When the men finished breakfast, they scattered
and dispersed. Salim was so organized that he
had nothing to do until lunch. Still, he stirred the
soups and stews, counted silverware, straightened
the napkins into neat piles. He rearranged the cold
drinks in the tub so the water was in one place,
the lemonade in another, the orange and cranberry
juices around the rim; it looked very appealing
when Salim was done.

While the men worked, Salim leaned against
his truck and looked out at the ocean. The lunch
hour whistle sounded and all of the workers came
back to eat. Once they were served, Salim stood
under the truck's awning and tried to stay cool.
The sun was very hot and Salim felt tired. Still, he
knew he would not sleep. During the four months
the project was stalled, Salim had stored sleep the
way bears store it in the winter; now that he was
working again, he would spend his nights pouring
over recipe books, testing out new dishes, cooking
big batches of old favorites. One thing that Salim
knew for sure was that buildings, no matter what
shape they were in, eventually got built. There
would come a time to sleep.

"You still open?" A young guy with a mustache
and an earring walked up to Salim's truck.

"He can't hear," one of the guys working near
Salim said.

The guy with the mustache started moving his
hands up and down, to mimic the opening of the
shutter on Salim's truck.

I can hear, Salim thought, and he opened the
shutter to prove it.

"Good job," this new guy said. "Can I get a
sandwich? I missed the lunch bell."

There were so many kinds of sandwiches. Salim
looked at the guy and thought, steak. He pulled out
a cheese steak and stuck it in the microwave. Then
he stuck in another one; Salim's sandwiches were
not small but this man seemed very hungry.

"Thanks, man," the guy said.

"He's deaf, I told you," the other guy said.

"No he's not," Pete McCoy was walking up
toward the truck. "He's not deaf, are you pal?"

Salim shook his head no.

"I remember you now," Pete said, "you were
here before we had to shut down. Your name's..."
and Pete paused until Salim pointed to the sign on
his truck.

"Yeah, right, Sauhl..im."

"I think it's more like Sah-leem," the new guy
said. "I was over there, man. I think they say it Sah-
leem."

It was Sah-leem. Salim put two bags of chips
up on the counter while the cheese steaks were
warming; he would give this guy one bag for free.

"Yeah, well, he ain't deaf," Pete said. "But he can't talk either. Isn't that right, guy? You can hear but you can't talk, right?"

Perhaps Habib would like to come here for a visit, Salim thought. He could go to the beach while Salim worked. Every single day he could lay in the warm sand, have a swim in the ocean, sip cold tea, read some books. When he picked his head up, he would see beautiful girls walking on the sand. Sometimes they would smile at him and then one day, one would walk right up and introduce herself. Habib would make room for her on his blanket and they would spend the day talking, Habib was a great talker. Habib would share his cold tea and before long, they would discover that they had a lot in common. Habib would invite her over for dinner and Salim and Habib would cook the specialty foods that Habib's mother cooked when they were growing up together in the house in Cleveland, the recipes she brought in her head when she took Salim and Habib to the United States to live, after the bombing. Habib's new friend would be so overwhelmed by the food and by the cousins' courteousness and generosity that she would invite them to dinner for the next night. Salim would bring chocolates, and Habib would bring flowers and wine. It would not be long, then, until Habib fell so in love with his friend and with Miami that he would want to live here forever, so he would get married and buy a house in Salim's neighborhood. In the evenings, the three of them might take drives together, looking at people's houses and imagining

what their lives were like. Together, he and Habib
would plan recipes and cook the kind of food
men like this who make strong buildings need and
want to eat. If Habib were here, his life would be
better than it was in Cleveland. And warmer. Salim
remembered how cold it was in Cleveland. He
remembered how cold the hospital room was when
his aunt took him there, how sad she looked when
the doctors said they could not help Salim. Even
though Salim was very little then, he remembered
the words for cold and tired and pain in his native
language but once they took his blanket away from
his throat, no sounds could ever come out. He had
never seen that blanket again. Perhaps when he got
home later, Salim would write his cousin a letter
and suggest he make a visit. Salim wrote very good
letters.

When Salim had cleaned everything up and
pulled the shutters down on his truck, he stopped
to listen to the sounds around him, familiar sounds
like drills and hammers, cranes creaking, the men
all shouting things to each other. Sounds that made
him feel happy and at home. Just in front of him,
Joe was measuring something that Salim thought
might be a door.

"Hey, Bub," a worker called from a low level
roof above where Joe was standing.

"Toss me up that cable, will ya?" Joe tossed
the cable up and Salim was thinking, That is not
Bub: it is Joe. Joe Palumbo. He has been working
for Pete McCoy for fifteen years. He lives in my
neighborhood, on McDonald Street, with his wife,

Nadine. She calls Joe here all the time.

Once, Salim saw them taking a walk through his neighborhood with their small son and he followed them and saw where they lived. Nadine has dark brown hair and is very pretty. Very pretty and sweet and nice; she was a good mother, Salim could tell because he saw how Nadine held her son's small hand while they walked but let her son go when he saw a butterfly he wanted to chase or a flower he wanted to touch. Joe and Nadine do not have any children now because the little boy died when their house caught fire a year after Salim knew who they were. It was in the newspaper. No one ever got over it. That is why Joe must build buildings and Nadine must call. All the time. It is very sad.

The Customer

Mrs. Fierstein and her daughter sat down at a table next to Ellen's. They were fully clothed even though it was 90 degrees outside and they were at the pool. Mrs. Fierstein's daughter, who was 62 years old and went by the name of Theresa, even though her mother had named her Dolores, motioned for the pool attendant to come over and put an umbrella up at their table. When the pool attendant was finished, Mrs. Fierstein tried to give her fifty cents but the attendant politely refused; people who worked at the condominium didn't take tips, no matter how small.

Ellen was watching the whole thing, not because she was interested but because the Fiersteins were too loud to ignore. Although she didn't think they looked particularly rich, Ellen wondered if they were because they had that way of behaving in public—of acting as if they were the only people in a space and the only people who mattered—that she'd seen in lots of rich people since she'd moved to Miami.

Before they arrived, Ellen had been alternating between reading a novel and looking out at the ocean. She had been in Miami Beach a year but she still felt a thrill inside every time she looked at the ocean and realized it was her backyard. She wished

her mother would consent to come and visit: their
farm was beautiful to be sure and Ellen missed the
long fields and the way the sun set over them, but
Ellen's mother had never seen the ocean and Ellen
knew she would fall in love with it.

The Fierstein's were arguing about who should
sit where. Ellen tried to look away. She had put up
her own umbrella; she had also brought the pool
attendant, whose name was Marisel, some muffins
and a bottle of cold water: Ellen was a personal
chef and brought food to the people who worked in
her building all the time.

Even though it was so hot, Ellen was determined
to stay outside a little longer because it was
Saturday and her only day off. She shopped and
cooked for two families Monday through Friday
and cooked and packaged five meals on Sunday
mornings, so the third family she worked for could
pick up their food at noon. In some ways, growing
up on a farm had prepared her well for this kind of
work, for having to make sacrifices to get the work
done, for taking care of other people. But there was
something deep and profound missing from the
hard work and care-taking she did in Miami: it was
the difference between gratitude and expectation.
In Wisconsin, everyone pitched in and worked hard
and even though it was her family, there was still
always a clear sense of appreciation. But in the
personal chef world, Ellen provided a service and
was paid for it. Maybe her clients were grateful for
her menu ideas, for the careful way she balanced
nutrition and flair, for the way her food tasted and

her attention to presentation. But if they were, Ellen didn't know because they never said anything. She was learning a lot in Miami, and not just about cooking.

There was actually a breeze coming off the ocean and with that and the shade from her umbrella, it was pleasant. She was reading a great novel called Boomerang and she wanted to write to the author and say, so I guess you can go home again, though that was something Ellen didn't believe could happen anywhere outside of a novel, not in the way you'd want it to.

Just when the main character was about to get on a train that would take her back to the family estate, the Fiersteins had arrived and caused so much commotion that Ellen gave up the book and watched them instead. Dolores/Theresa called her mother "Ma" and shouted as if the old woman was in Ft. Lauderdale, instead of at the table beside her. She said, "Ma, sit over there. Out of the sun. Are you crazy? It's 90 degrees" and the mother said, "Dolores, where would I sit out of the sun?" and that's when the daughter waved Marisel over for an umbrella, but not before she said, "My name's Theresa, Ma, Jesus Christ" and the mother said, "Don't say that, Dolores. Don't say Jesus Christ."

Once the umbrella was in place and Marisel had gone back to her seat under a palm tree, a big breeze came across the pool area and Mrs. Fierstein said quite loudly, "Now that's a breeze." "It's a breeze, Ma," her daughter said, as if there were no cause for celebrating it. Theresa was a big

woman and she wore white Capri pants that were
too small and a halter-type top that was too young.
Her mother was dressed to the nines: linen shift,
matching jacket with a butterfly pin at the lapel and
a pillbox hat with a thin meshy veil falling at her
forehead. Ellen could see that Mrs. Fierstein was
one of those women for whom tradition mattered,
for whom it meant something to get dressed up.

But it was too hot for the clothes she was
wearing and Ellen got warmer just looking at her.
But then another big breeze came. It came right
behind Ellen and twirled around her neck. Then it
lifted up under her umbrella, making it shake, and
then under the Fierstein's umbrella, making it take
flight. In a second, it was out of its stand in the
table and flying across the pool patio.

"Jesus Christ," Theresa yelled and the mother
said "Dolores, don't say that!" and Ellen was
already up. She chased the huge umbrella as it
rolled past unsuspecting sunbathers and finally
caught it just before it reached the glass wall that
separated the condominium pool area from the
beach. Her heart was thumping because it had all
happened so fast and seemed so dire but once she
got a good hold on it, she calmed down and began
the arduous process of dragging it over to Marisel,
who had somehow missed the whole thing.

"Thanks," Marisel said, when she realized why
Ellen was standing in front of her with an umbrella.
"You want fifty cents?" They both started laughing
and Ellen patted her on the shoulder and turned
to go back to her table where, while she was being

heroic, Mrs. Fierstein and her daughter had joined her. The mother had taken Ellen's chair and was sitting on Ellen's towel, while Theresa had pulled her own chair over. They had moved Ellen's book and water bottle to make room for their oversize purses.

"You don't mind," Theresa said, as if it was statement instead of a question. Ellen looked around; she had no chair.

"Oh, I gave my mother your chair. She's 95. It's hot out here. You don't mind."

"No, of course not," Ellen said, because it was her way. She pulled another chair to the table and sat down.

"I'm Theresa Fierstein and this my mother, Mrs. Fierstein."

"I named her Dolores, Dolores Pearl Fierstein, but now she's Theresa."

"Cut it out, Ma," Theresa said.

"I'm Ellen," Ellen said, "nice to meet you."

"Helen, that's not a Jewish name, is it?" Mrs. Fierstein asked.

"I don't know," Ellen said, "but my family's not Jewish."

"Mine is," the mother said, "but now we have a shiksa daughter named Theresa."

Theresa rolled her eyes. "We're not staying long. We're going to lunch at the Carillon at 1:00 but I needed some sun first. I work too hard, never get outside."

"Isn't it a little hot for your mother out here, all dressed up?" Ellen asked, worrying that a 95 year old woman fully-clothed in the sun could faint in the heat. Ellen had a momentary flash of her own grandmother, who was 85 and had spent most of her life in a sleeveless blouse in a hot kitchen or on her knees in a hot garden but who now spent her summers sitting in front of the window air conditioner on her farm in Wisconsin.

"My mother's lived here for 75 years," Theresa said, "and these are her clothes."

"Seventy-five years," Mrs. Fierstein said, "my husband died three years ago."

Ellen didn't know how to respond. She lived alone, didn't know many people in Miami and wasn't good at small talk, which was great in Miami since most people spoke Spanish—which she did not—so she just smiled. But smiling at the news that someone's husband died didn't seem appropriate so she said, "Oh, I'm sorry."

"His own fault," Mrs. Fierstein said, "Smoking. It killed him. And weight. He was fat as a house," and then she looked at her daughter and smirked. This was a bit too much information for Ellen, who really wanted just to relax and read her book.

"Where do you live?" Theresa asked.

"Here," Ellen said, pointing to the condo building.

"What floor?"

"Six."

"So does my mother," she said.

"Why haven't I seen you?" Mrs. Fierstein wanted to know. "You're a pretty girl. A nice girl. Why don't I know you?"

"I don't know," Ellen said, "I leave early for
work and when I get home, I don't go out much. I
am usually working."

"What do you do?" Theresa asked but before
Ellen could answer, she said, "I'm an accountant."

"She makes a lot of money," her mother said.

"Not so much, Ma. Shhh. Don't say that. Next
thing you know, someone'll rob me."

"Seems unlikely here," Ellen said. The residents
of their condominium were mostly upper class,
well-off people.

"You don't know," Theresa snapped. "A lot of
these people," she was whispering now and using
her arm to indicate the rest of the people at the
pool, "they're just on vacation, renting the condos
out. You don't know who they are."

You don't know who I am, Ellen thought, The
idea of stealing Theresa's purse flashed through her
mind. But it was a huge purse, like a small suitcase,
and Ellen didn't think she could fit it into her beach
bag.

"They seem decent enough," Ellen said. She
had no idea why she was even participating in
this conversation except that these women had
planted themselves at her table and, she had to
admit, even though Mrs. Fierstein was nothing like
her own quiet, humble, shy grandmother, she did
have a fondness for old people because she was so
homesick. But, still, she wanted these women to get
to their lunch so she could get back to her book.
She looked at her watch. It was only 12:15.

"Where's the Carillon? Is it far?" Ellen asked,

hoping it was so they would leave. She'd never heard of that restaurant before.

"Just up North a little," Theresa said. "We're taking a cab. It's nice...it's a..."

"It's a home for old people," her mother shouted, "my daughter is trying to get me in a home for old people."

"So it's a home, so what?" Theresa said. "It has a nice restaurant. You might like it. They have chicken salad in the pineapple there. You love that."

"Not if the pineapple is too soft," Mrs. Fierstein said, "and not if the chicken salad has celery. Does it? Does that chicken have celery in it there?"

"I don't know Ma, we'll see. We'll see. If it does, you'll pick it out."

"Pick it out," the mother said, with a big tsk that was more like a curse.

"So what do you do?" Theresa asked Ellen again.

"I'm a..." and she was about to say personal chef when Mrs. Fierstein said, "Studio or there is a bedroom?"

"What?" her daughter said.

"I'm not talking to you. I'm talking to..."

"Ellen," Ellen said.

"Yes, Helen. I'm talking to Helen. You live in a studio or there is a bedroom?"

"A studio."

"Ah, well, you come to my apartment tomorrow. See the room."

"What room, Ma? Consuela's room?"

"Consuela. She's a pig," Mrs. Fierstein said.

"She is not, Ma. She's a nice person."

"How would you know? You're never there."

"I'm here now, aren't I?"

"To take me to the home, you are."

Ellen looked at her watch again but she knew only a couple of minutes had gone by. There were lots of relaxing things she could do in her studio on her day off—take a bath, call her cousin in Iowa, stretch out on her mat, lay on the couch and finish her novel. She felt bad for Mrs. Fierstein, sitting out at the pool all dressed up and knowing her daughter wanted to put her in a home. But what could Ellen do? She pulled her beach bag from the ground and reached for the novel, to put it inside.

"Consuela stays with my mother at night. She comes at 5:00 and leaves at 8:00 in the morning. She's a nice person."

"What do you know about a nice person?" her mother said. "What do you know? Here, this girl?" and she pointed to Ellen, "she is a nice person."

Ellen smiled. She was a nice person and had always been a good girl because she had been raised to be a good girl. She did well all through school and in the early mornings and on weekends, she helped out on the family farms, her own family's and her grandparent's next door. Her friends all had the same life and found time to do the things farm kids do—hang out at the lake, drive into town for the movies, drink beers in someone's barn. When she finished high school, she knew her parents couldn't afford to send her to college but she didn't mind: she loved being home and working on the

farm and she could always read on her own. After
graduating, she had more serious responsibilities on
the farm and then in the kitchen: she became like
an apprentice to her mother and grandmother and
learned how to cook.

Ellen thanked Mrs. Fierstein for saying she was
a nice girl and continued to pack up her things.
There was a water bottle, her watch, a pair of
goggles she had used when she swam her laps. Mrs.
Fierstein was still sitting on her towel but Ellen
didn't know how to disturb her so she decided to
leave the towel there.

"You'll see the room," Mrs. Fierstein said to
Ellen, when she noticed Ellen getting ready to leave,
"it's a beautiful room. Consuela is a pig. You are a
nice girl."

"Ellen isn't going to live with you, Ma, so just
forget it, ok?"

"Then you live with me, Dolores. I'm not going
to an old folks home."

"Well," Ellen said, now that everything was in
her bag and she was standing up, "it was nice to
meet both of you. I hope you have nice lunch."

"Wait," Theresa commanded, "you never told
me what you do."

Startled by her thwarted attempt to get away,
Ellen said, "I'm a personal chef" and just as she was
about to leave, Theresa said, "What? Did you hear
that, Ma? A chef. I knew it. This is our lucky day.
Sit down. We have to talk."

Obediently, Ellen sat back down.

"My mother is having a Fourth of July dinner,

at her apartment. For our family and some of her friends. Her apartment is just down the hall from yours. You can do it. Like a picnic. Picnic food, so I don't have to go to Publix and get it all myself."

"Sure, I can do that," Ellen said, "I grew up on picnics." Holidays were huge events in Ellen's family and for each one she and her mother and grandmother and all the aunts and cousins would prepare the best food made from things they raised and grew on their farms. Ellen's clients in Miami were all on the Atkins Diet or the South Beach Diet or wanting the upscale, complex dishes she'd learned to make at the culinary school. There was nothing Ellen would like more than to cook a real Fourth of July picnic, the kind her family always made. And if she took this job, she'd have some extra money for presents to take when she went home for a visit in August.

"Fine, how much?" Theresa wanted to know.

"It depends," Ellen answered, "on how many people you're having, if you want me to serve it, if I need to hire people to help me..."

"Not that I'm paying for it," Theresa said, pointing to her mother, "she is...and maybe my sister Bertie will kick some money in."

"Bertha," Mrs. Fierstein said.

"Yeah, Ma, you gave us some great names, didn't you? Dolores and Bertha."

"Bertha loves her name. They're good names for Jewish girls, but what would you know with your Theresa and your swearing."

"Ma," Theresa said. "Do you want Ellen to do

your Fourth of July party or not?"

"Sure, sure, she'll come over and see the room. Sure."

"I can suggest some dishes that would be good," Ellen said. She had not brought paper with her to the pool but she had a pen in her bag and pulled it out; she pulled the novel out too, to make notes for this party on the back of the cover.

"Consuela, she'll do the dishes," Mrs. Fierstein said.

"Food, Ma, she's talking about food not dishes." But Mrs. Fierstein was looking out at the ocean now so her daughter said, "Make some chicken; my mother doesn't like it dry. Whatever goes with that, I don't know. Can you make some dessert?"

"Of course," Ellen said, "like mixed berry shortcake, red white and blue for the Fourth?"

"Shortcake, goyim," Mrs. Fierstein said.

"Goyim?" Ellen said. It was a word that sounded familiar but she didn't think she knew what it meant.

"Goyim, means not Jewish."

"Oh," Ellen said. "You want a Jewish dessert?" not that she knew what that would be.

"Fourth of July isn't a Jewish holiday, Ma," Theresa said. Then she turned to Ellen. "Make a pie. Get the can of whip cream."

"OK," Ellen said, writing everything down but thinking about her mother's fried chicken, her grandmother's apple-peach cobbler with homemade vanilla bean ice cream.

"So how much?" Theresa asked again.

188Diane Goodman

"Well..." Ellen tried to do some quick calculations in her head. "I guess around $15.00 a person but I'll have to go home and figure it all out and then I'll call you with a final price."

"You'll come tomorrow and see the room and you'll give the price," Mrs. Fierstein said. Other than being 95 and probably not too sure on her feet, Mrs. Fierstein seemed pretty sharp. She knew what she wanted. And what she didn't want, which was to go an old folks home.

"Sure. What's your apartment number?"

"She's in 612," Theresa said. "You go at 1:00. 1:00 is a good time for her."

"Me, too," Ellen said, since her Sunday clients came to get their food at noon. She stood up and picked up her things. "See you then," she said.

"You won't see me," Theresa said.

"Who does?" Mrs. Fierstein said, "you're never here."

"I'm here now, Ma, aren't I?"

"Yeah, to take me to the home," her mother said. "Nothing worse than an ungrateful daughter, Helen. You're a good girl. I know."

"Her name's Ellen, Ma," Theresa said.

"She knows what I mean," Mrs. Fierstein said, and nodded her head in Ellen's direction.

* * *

When Ellen got to 612 on Sunday at 1:00, the door was already open. Ellen knocked anyway but no one answered. Then she heard Mrs. Fierstein on the phone.

"She'll come, she'll come," Mrs. Fierstein was

saying.

"I'm here," Ellen yelled into the apartment.

"See? She's here," Mrs. Fierstein said and hanging up the phone called out, "Come in, dear."

The apartment, while neat and clean, was garish. There were two couches in the small living room that had nothing to do with each other. One was rust-colored crush velvet, patches worn down to white on the cushions and arm rests. The other couch was smaller, puffy, and covered with what looked like a handmade crocheted blanket, in screaming colors of magenta, lime, tangerine and then covered again in plastic. A huge banana-leaf tree had reached the ceiling and for some time, had been forced to grow downward and created a kind of jungle shadow. Paper plates were stacked on the dining room table, which was also in the living room; in a line next to the table were an old yellow bean bag chair, a director's chair with a parrot pattern on the fabric, two high stools covered in broken leather and topped with newspapers. The apartment was furnished with old discarded items, things her daughters must have outgrown or tired of when they were much younger women. Ellen wondered how Theresa could let her mother live like this. Ellen's mother's house was warm with earth-colored furniture, fresh flowers on all the tables, checkered curtains her mother had made, books in the bookshelf, music usually playing. Her grandmother's house was the same except her grandmother loved blue. All shades of blues. The families never had much money and as Ellen got

older, it seemed to her that no matter how hard her
parents worked, there was never enough money.
No one ever got anything new unless it was farm
equipment but still their houses were lovely, clean,
inviting homes.

But what all the homes had in common were
family photos on the walls. On Mrs. Fierstein's
walls, the photos were old, yellowed and hung
crookedly and Mrs. Fierstein, her arm clawing
Ellen's just under her armpit, insisted on showing
them all to her, identifying everyone in each picture.
It was a gallery of her family, generations and
generations. There were cousins and aunts and
uncles, rabbis and rabbis' wives and friends who
had died. The photos were so old and so badly
cared for that all the people looked exactly the
same, the men and the women, but each time Mrs.
Fierstein named one, she squeezed Ellen's arm
harder and Ellen looked closely at all the faces.

"And this is my granddaughter," Mrs. Fierstein
said, when she finally got to the last one. "Dolores's
daughter. She named her Morgan but I call her
Rebecca, my mother's name. She lives in New
York, my Rebecca, but she used to live here," Mrs.
Fierstein swept her free arm—the one that wasn't
entwined in Ellen's—around her apartment so
Ellen thought maybe Rebecca lived here with her
grandmother. "She's a nurse. A good girl. Like you."

The morning that Ellen was leaving for
Miami Beach, she went across the field to her
grandmother's house to say goodbye. Her
grandmother was the only person in her family still

speaking to her at the time. Her mother did not understand why she wanted to go all the way to Florida to learn the same things she was learning in her own kitchen. "What will I be saying to people who ask who you are?" her grandmother had said, pointing to a picture of Ellen waving from the tractor in one of her grandfather's fields. "You'll say I'm your granddaughter, Gran," Ellen had said, "who's going to Miami to learn how to be a famous chef." "I guess I will," her grandmother had said. And she had given Ellen a hundred dollars and a jar of homemade blueberry jam.

"Your granddaughter is beautiful," Ellen said to Mrs. Fierstein.

"She's a nurse, in New York," Mrs. Fierstein said again. "Come, see the room."

The room was the exact opposite of the rest of the apartment. It was white and bare looked as if it had recently been painted. In it, there was a single bed made up with white sheets but no blanket or spread or comforter, a small blonde dresser, no blinds or curtains on the window and a picture above the bed of a gull flying over the ocean.

"It's beautiful, no?" Mrs. Fierstein said. "And look," still arm in arm with Ellen, she moved them toward a door. "It has its own entrance, very private."

"Beautiful," Ellen said.

"You love it, don't you?" the old woman said.

"I love it," Ellen agreed, not sure if she should make it clear that she wouldn't be moving in or if she should just change the subject. "Would you like to talk about the Fourth of July party?" Ellen asked. "I have a menu all typed up and a final price."

Mrs. Fierstein nodded her head and moved herself and Ellen back into the living room. Then the phone rang.

"Well, did she show?" Ellen heard Theresa's voice on the other end of the phone; "I told you she was here," Mrs. Fierstein said. "What? You think she wouldn't come when she says she would come? Like someone I know?"

"I come, Ma, I come when I come. I just wanted to make sure she showed."

"Helen loves the room," Mrs. Fierstein said and hung up the phone.

Then she sat down at the dining room table and motioned for Ellen to join her.

Ellen pulled out two copies of the menu and invoice. She slid one over to Mrs. Fierstein.

"Fine, fine," Mrs. Fierstein said, without looking. "I'll pay. It will be me and my daughters, Dolores and Bertha, Bertha's boyfriend who she lives with but they're not married, their neighbor— poor woman, never goes anywhere—the neighbors down the hall. You know them? Mr. and Mrs. Jimenez. Old Cubans. They like a party. Maybe 8 people. You'll get some plastic cloths to go over this table."

"Sure," Ellen said. "So here's what I'll make and how much it will cost." She pointed to the paper.

"Fine, fine, I'll pay," Mrs. Fierstein said again, still not looking at the paper. "And Consuela will do the dishes. You'll serve the food. And you'll make me the food first, so I can taste."

Ellen wasn't sure what that meant so she said, "Pardon?"

"The food, you'll make it for me. First." Mrs. Fierstein was nodding her head as if this was a normal procedure when you hired a caterer. "You'll bring me...let's see, what is this?" Mrs. Fierstein pulled a pair of thick glasses out of her housecoat pocket and pulled the menu closer. "Fried chicken, baked potato salad—you bake the salad?...what's this? Cold green beans and tomatoes? I don't know that, you'll bring it first...biscuits, baked beans, the cobbler, like a pie?...you don't have to bring the ice cream first. But all the rest, so I can taste it."

Ellen had excelled at the culinary institute, just as she had thought she would when flipping through a magazine in the waiting room of her dentist's office, she saw an ad for a cooking school in Miami Beach. Being in Madison at the dentist was the farthest Ellen ever went away from home and the three hours it took to drive there, have her yearly check-up and drive back about the longest. But she tore the advertisement out of the magazine and stuck in her pocket anyway. She thought if she could take what she knew about cooking and become a professional chef, then she could make enough money to eventually come back home and ease up the burden on her family. Farming wasn't the way it used to be when her parents were young: they worked and worked and struggled so much, especially when equipment broke or unpredictable weather—long draughts or too much rain—

postponed or sometimes even destroyed the harvest.
Her parents weren't getting any younger and her
grandmother was now too old to do the hard farm
work. So secretly Ellen applied to the school as a
scholarship student and when she was accepted,
she spent the three months before she left trying
to convince her mother that it was the right thing
to do. The program was only six months long and
after graduating, the school guaranteed immediate
employment at rates Ellen could not believe were
possible.

But it was true. In the six months since
graduation, Ellen had made and saved more money
than the family farm brought in the year before.
She knew her parents, and her grandmother,
worried about her being on her own in a place
like Miami but everything that Ellen had imagined
would happen was happening. One more year
of cooking elegant dinners, the South Beach diet,
portable foods for family airplanes, and elaborate
hors d'oeuvres for splashy cocktail parties, and she
would be able to go home and make life easier for
everyone there. Until then, she had to withstand the
suffering. Her mother didn't understand how lonely
she was, how desperate to return home, because her
mother could not reconcile the idea of leaving with
the idea of wanting to be home.

At the school, Ellen had learned how to cook
the range of things customers might like—roasts
and duckling and lamb chops, terrines and
cassoulets, sauces and salads, dozens of kinds
of potatoes and risottos, European cakes and

complicated tarts. But the cooking Ellen was best at, the foods that meant the most to her, were the ones she'd learned to cook from her mother and grandmother on the farm, the ones that made up this Fourth of July menu. The foods Ellen wanted to make for Mrs. Fierstein's party were foods she hadn't eaten for a year, foods that she wanted and needed to make. Right away.

"Yes, yes I will make all these for you ," Ellen said, "in fact, I'll bring them all over later today." Mrs. Fierstein was still looking at the menu but Ellen was already thinking that she could go to and be back from the store by 2:00, that by 3:00 her kitchen would start smelling like home. "I'll make all these foods for you, Mrs. Fierstein, so you can taste them. I can bring them over by 6:00. My own grandmother taught me how to make these things."

"My granddaughter lives in New York," Mrs. Fierstein said.

* * *

The line was busy the first time Ellen tried her mother so she went back to snipping the ends off the green beans. Chopped fresh tomatoes were draining in the sink and the chicken was soaking in buttermilk. She thought she'd prep the rest of the food—slice the apples and peaches for the cobbler, let the baked potatoes cool so she could dice them, mince onion, season the flour for frying—and then try her mother again. An hour later, the phone was ringing and two seconds later, Ellen heard her mother's voice.

"Hi, Mom."

Her mother didn't respond so Ellen said, "It's me, Mom. Ellen."

"I know," her mother said, and Ellen thought she heard her mother's voice crack, was sure she could see her sitting up straight in the kitchen chair and rubbing her cheek with her free hand.

"How are you, Mom?"

"I'm good, good," her mother said. "You?"

"Good, fine. Um, I'm excited about seeing you this summer."

"Us too, Ellen. What do you look like now? I see pictures of girls in Miami. Are you skinny now?"

Ellen had always been skinny, all her life.

"Sure, Mom, same as always. You know what I look like. It hasn't been that long."

"A year is a long time."

"I know, Mom; I wish you and Dad and Gran had used those tickets I bought for you at Christmas."

"Christmas is the time to be home, Ellen, not to leave home," her mother said and then before Ellen could explain, again, that she made most of her money during the holiday season in Miami, her mother said, "Why are you calling now? Is something wrong?"

"No, everything's fine. I just miss you, that's all."

"You could have stayed here, with us, Ellen. We needed you here. We needed you here more than we need money." Ellen knew her mother missed her but that she could not help but punish her as well.

"But it helps, Mom, doesn't it, the money I send?" Ellen said.

"You know it does." Her mother paused. "You're sure everything is ok?"

"Yes, fine. But I need some cooking advice."

"From me?" her mother said. "What can I tell you, Ellen? You went to cooking school. I'm sure they taught you things I don't know. You know how to cook." Every phone call since Ellen had left was a volley between something kind and something that stung.

"But not your foods, Mom," Ellen tried again. "I want to make the things you and Gran do. I have a new client. She's a 95 year old lady. She wants to have a Fourth of July picnic party for her daughters and some friends. I wanted to go over some stuff with you." Even though those recipes were stamped into Ellen's head and she could make all those dishes with her eyes closed, she wanted to hear her mother say the words. She wanted to hear her mother tell her to pat the chicken dry before shaking it in the seasoned flour in a paper bag, to remember to slice the apples and peaches as thinly as she could, not to add extra onion to the potatoes, to let the tomatoes drain out completely before mixing them into the steamed beans.

"Why are you doing this?"

"Doing what?"

"This, this Ellen."

"You don't return my calls, Mom."

"I don't have anything to say. You know what goes on here. It doesn't change. You lived here all

your life. We don't have money to spend telling you
what you already know."

"Do you miss me, Mom?"

There was a silence that lasted a few seconds
and then Ellen's mother said, "You're a silly girl,
Ellen."

Mrs. Fierstein kept calling Ellen a nice girl.
Moving alone to a crazy place like Miami Beach
from a safe normal place like rural Wisconsin, that's
not what silly girls did. It's what nice girls did, nice
girls who knew that what they were doing would
be right for everyone, even though there were some
temporary sacrifices to be made along the way.

"How's Dad?" Ellen managed to choke out.

"Your father went to the store about half an
hour ago, " Ellen's mother said, "to get me some
flour. I need to make a pie. Your Gran is coming for
supper."

"What are you making?" Ellen asked, trying not
to cry.

"Pot roast."

"Brussel sprouts?" Ellen could smell the rich pot
roast gravy, see the butter melting on the vegetables.

"No. Your father can't eat those anymore. Don't
agree with him. I'll put some beans in from the
garden."

Ellen looked at her bowl of snipped beans.

"I was thinking of putting some bacon in that
cold green bean and tomato salad you make. What
do you think?"

"I think it's good the way it is," her mother said.

* * *

By 6:00, Ellen had placed fried chicken, potato salad, green beans with tomatoes, baked beans, homemade biscuits with some of her Gran's blueberry jam, and warm cobbler on a big silver tray. She decorated the tray with baby's breath and tiny yellow chrysanthemums, and sprinkled some gold star confetti she had leftover from a catering all around the flowers. She looked at the food was proud. Her mother would be proud of her, too, if she wasn't so angry.

This time, Mrs. Fierstein's door wasn't open so Ellen balanced the tray on one arm and knocked. It took several knocks and then finally a Latina woman in a maid's uniform answered the door. Consuela.

"Can I help you?" she asked Ellen. She was in her fifties and looked tired, maybe annoyed. Her voice was stiff, not welcoming.

"Hi, I'm Ellen, I live down the hall. I'm catering Mrs. Fierstein's party on the Fourth of July and she wanted to try the menu first so I made all the dishes. Here they are. She's expecting me."

"I know who you are," Consuela said, and then seemed as if she was going to say something else but she just stood there, silent.

Ellen felt an immediate kinship with Consuela; she understood her need to be professional because Ellen conducted herself this way when at her clients' homes. She and Consuela would be working together on the Fourth of July; she would help her with the dishes.

"There's enough here for both of you," Ellen

said, "I hope you like it."

"So you love my room," Consuela said. "You live down the hall but you love my room."

"Your room is nice," Ellen said in a low conspiratorial voice, "but I'm not moving into it. I have my own apartment, you're right. I'm just a cook. That's all."

"That's all," Consuela said, as if she didn't believe Ellen, and turned to walk into the apartment. Ellen followed and with her foot, kicked the door closed. Mrs. Fierstein was sitting at her dining room table.

"Hi," Ellen said.

"Helen. Helen is here," she said to Consuela. "I hope your room is clean. Helen might need to see it again."

"No, I don't need to see the room," Ellen said, the tray weighing more heavily in her hands now as she stood between the now obviously chilly Consuela and Mrs. Fierstein's misguided notion. "I'm just here to deliver the food. I brought you the food."

Now Mrs. Fierstein looked at her as if she was a total stranger.

"What food?" Mrs. Fierstein said, eyeing the tray skeptically.

"The sample food, for the Fourth of July?"

"It's not the Fourth of July."

Ellen just stared at her. Although old and a little batty, Mrs. Fierstein had seemed perfectly cogent and coherent during both of their earlier conversations. And she had just been there that afternoon.

"I know. That's a few weeks away. But when I was over earlier, you asked me to make you all the foods I planned to cook for your party. Remember? I made them. Here they are."

"Do I have to pay for this?"

Ellen had planned on tacking the cost for the sample foods onto the final bill but she said, "No, of course not. It's a gift."

"A gift," Mrs. Fierstein snorted. "Put it down here."

Ellen set the tray down and backed up beside Consuela. Consuela moved away. Ellen's grandmother's jam was shiny, steam was still rising off the biscuits, which she'd baked in heart-shaped muffin tins. She'd sprinkled grated lemon zest over the chicken, carved roses out of cherry tomatoes to garnish the green beans, stuck slices of hard-cooked eggs all around the potato salad bowl with clumps of parsley in between them. The tray looked so beautiful, so professional. And suddenly Ellen knew that if her mother saw this version of the comfort foods she'd been making for years, she wouldn't be proud of her daughter at all.

"I thought you said you were going to make this," Mrs. Fierstein said.

"I did," Ellen answered, confused. "I made all of it, right there." She pointed to the tray. "Except the jam...that's my grandmother's jam. She makes it from blueberries she grows herself."

"Where did this come from?" Mrs. Fierstein asked but this time she was looking at Consuela.

"The girl brought it," Consuela said, "the girl who loves my room. Just now. She brought it."

"But from where?" Mrs. Fierstein said, her voice getting a bit louder.

"Where did you bring this from?" Consuela asked.

"From my apartment," Ellen said, helplessly. "From my kitchen. I made it."

"She made it, in her kitchen, her own kitchen, that she has down the hall," Consuela told Mrs. Fierstein, as if Ellen wasn't even there.

"Did you get the plastic tablecloths, too?" Mrs. Fierstein said.

"Um no, I didn't, not yet," Ellen said. "I'll get them when I go to the store to shop for the party."

"You didn't shop? At the store? So where did you get all this? From a restaurant?"

"I hope you like it," Ellen said weakly and left Mrs. Fierstein's apartment.

* * *

"We have a problem," Theresa said, when Ellen picked up her ringing phone the next afternoon around 3:00 and said hello. She had just come back from the grocery store.

"Who is this?" Ellen asked.

"It's Theresa Fierstein, Mrs. Fierstein's daughter. We have a problem."

"What sort of problem?" Ellen asked, though she thought she already knew.

"My mother thinks you sublet your food."

"What?"

"My mother thinks you sublet your food...you

know, that you get it at a restaurant and then sell it to people."

"That's preposterous," Ellen said.

"Well, that's what she thinks. She thinks you don't know what a Fourth of July party is, that you don't know a picnic."

"I grew up on a farm, Theresa," Ellen said defensively. "In the country. I grew up eating picnic food on the Fourth of July, the same food I brought your mother. Those were my mother's recipes, and my grandmother's."

"So your mother makes fancy flowers out of tomatoes?"

"No, she doesn't, of course not," Ellen said, thinking of her mother's food and how its hominess made it beautiful on its own. "But I'm a caterer. You're paying for this food. I make it look like it deserves to be paid for."

"I'm not paying for it, she is," Theresa said, referring to her mother, "but what do you mean paying for it? She said you weren't charging her for that."

"I'm not...I'm not charging her for that," Ellen stammered, "just for the regular dinner, on the Fourth. But I wanted her to see what it would look like."

"Well, she did. And she also said you didn't like it."

"Didn't like it? What? The food? The food that I made?"

"No, the room. She said you didn't like the room."

Ellen didn't know what to say. "I don't think I know what you're talking about," Ellen said.

"Consuela's room. She said you didn't like it."

"I told her I loved, it, that it was beautiful," Ellen said, remembering.

"But Conseula told her you had your own apartment. "

"Of course I have my own apartment," Ellen said, the level of her exasperation rising fast. "You know that. Besides, your mother showed me the room but she didn't ask me to live in it..."

"So you would've?" Theresa interrupted.

"No," Ellen said, "I can't live in that room. I have my own apartment. But she didn't ask me to. She just showed me the room and then asked me to make the Fourth of July menu for her so she could taste it. I cooked all day for her yesterday, I made all the foods."

"Like I said, we have a problem. She thought you loved the room. And I thought, well, I didn't know but my mother hated the Carillon and she told Consuela you were going to move into the room."

"Why would she tell Consuela that?" Ellen asked. "I never said I would live there. And at the pool on Saturday, even you told your mother I wouldn't do that."

"Since when does she listen to me?"

The conversation was becoming more and more surreal. Ellen wanted to hang up but she was too polite.

"So now what?" Ellen said.

"I tasted your chicken. It was pretty good."

"It's very good," Ellen heard herself saying, "it's a recipe that's been in my family for generations. My mother has won prizes for that chicken at the fair."

"Does your mother's have those little yellow things on it?"

"That's just lemon zest. Just lemon peel, that's all."

"Well, it threw my mother for a loop, I can tell you that. She thinks chicken is supposed to be soft, baked or boiled like soup chicken. She doesn't understand zest or peel or whatever you call it. Or the little roses you made from those tomatoes. She doesn't want to pay you for restaurant food."

But I made that food, Ellen was going to say, until she realized it was pointless.

"Fine," Ellen said. "I understand. If you could return my tray, just leave it outside my door, that would be great."

"Why don't you just get it when you drop off the plastic table cloths?"

Ellen looked up and saw the two plastic tablecloths she'd bought that afternoon for Mrs. Fierstein on her counter.

"I didn't get the tablecloths," Ellen said.

"Oh, ok. We'll get them at the grocery when we go get the food for the Fourth of July. They have good wings there, regular potato salad—it comes in those plastic containers—and they make apple pies that taste like homemade. My mother likes that pie. She always says she doesn't but then she eats two

pieces of it. Ha! Consuela will do the dishes. Don't
worry about it."

But that wasn't what Ellen was worried about.
Mrs. Fierstein was Theresa Fierstein's mother.
Consuela had a clean white room and would do
as many dishes as there were to do. Ellen's mother
would be as likely to put bacon on her green bean
salad as she would be to walk half way across the
country to bring her only daughter home. Ellen had
missed it entirely. Now she was only worried that
she had figured it out in time.

The Cook

The fish counter is at the top of the canned goods aisle so even though I only buy fresh fruit and vegetables for my customers, because they would raise their eyebrows at anything else, I hang out in the canned goods because I have a crush on the fish man and sometimes he's not at the counter when I am ready to go there. I pretend to study things in cans my customers would never eat— potatoes, corn, kidney beans—but every couple of seconds I am looking up at the fish counter and when I see the fish man is there, I grab my cart and make my way to him. He always gives me the best fish at the best price and a lot of times he asks me what I'm making that day and sometimes says my hair looks nice. Sometimes it does. I collect barrettes.

But today there is a guy just ahead of me in the canned goods aisle and he is blocking my view. I try to look over his shoulder and his scrawny body but for some reason I can't understand he is moving really fast, almost like he's dancing, so when I try to move too so I can see the fish counter, he's always right in front of me. I think I'll pass him, just a little, so I can get a better look but when I get ready to go, I look up and see he is staring right through my eyes.

The fish counter is at the top of the canned goods aisle so even though I only buy fresh fruit and vegetables for my customers, because they would raise their eyebrows at anything else, I hang out in the canned goods because I have a crush on the fish man and sometimes he's not at the counter when I am ready to go there. I pretend to study things in cans my customers would never eat— potatoes, corn, kidney beans—but every couple of seconds I am looking up at the fish counter and when I see the fish man is there, I grab my cart and make my way to him. He always gives me the best fish at the best price and a lot of times he asks me what I'm making that day and sometimes says my hair looks nice. Sometimes it does. I collect barrettes.

But today there is a guy just ahead of me in the canned goods aisle and he is blocking my view. I try to look over his shoulder and his scrawny body but for some reason I can't understand he is moving really fast, almost like he's dancing, so when I try to move too so I can see the fish counter, he's always right in front of me. I think I'll pass him, just a little, so I can get a better look but when I get ready to go, I look up and see he is staring right through my eyes.

He isn't the most handsome guy I've ever seen. He's tall and too skinny and he blinks so much that I can't even tell what color his eyes are. But he's got that kind of buzz haircut that looks good on young guys so I look back at him and I smile.

I won't say he frowned, exactly. He just stared.

That's ok. I'm used to two things here: I'm used to being stared at and I'm used to being ignored. Most of the girls here are ultra-skinny and ultra-beautiful so if you're a big plain girl like me, people either look hard at you because they don't understand or they don't see you at all. It's true with all the strangers, for sure. And the people I work for? They wouldn't care if I was Jennifer Lopez (though sometimes I wonder what they would do if I was).

So when this buzz cut guy gives me what we used to call in high school "the hairy eyeball," like he thinks he's scaring me or something, I just shrug my shoulders, grab my cart and go. I'm making bouillabaisse for Mrs. Wallace today and that means that I have to spend a lot of time at the fish counter, ordering all the seafood that you have to have to make a really good bouilliabaisse.

If women liked to cook or could admit they liked to eat, I wouldn't have a job. Or at least not this one. I am a cook. My clients calls me a "private chef" but believe me, that sounds a lot more glamorous than it is. Nowadays, I spend most of my time doing other people's grocery shopping and then I take it to big houses and in big kitchens I cook food. Well, it's what some people would call food, I guess. Mostly I am broiling things like skinless chicken breasts without oil or butter or breadcrumbs or sauce, or cooking the Atkins Diet or the South Beach Diet or whatever diet anyone comes up with that promises you can be skinny in no time. I live in Miami Beach; that should explain it.

One thing I've learned is that there is a big
difference between being a cook and being a chef. I
went to chef school, where I learned how to make
things like daube de boeuf, vacherin, African lamb
stew, salt crusted shrimp with wasabi mayonaisse.
Now that's cooking. It takes me no time to hand-
whip egg whites so they'll stand straight up; mine
are so stiff that they'd probably salute you if I
didn't have to right away fold them into something
else. Being a chef is like being an artist: you have
ingredients and you have a vision and most of
the time you don't know how the two will come
together. You don't know what will happen but
then something amazing happens and you know
you can never do it the same way again but it
doesn't matter. Next time you'll do something else.
Something bigger and better. It's hard to explain
and I don't try to. I've never really met anyone who
could understand.

To be a great chef, you need patience and
imagination and then when whatever you're
making is done, you look around the kitchen
for something else to make your dish almost too
beautiful to eat. You mince some basil or go out in
the garden and pluck some tiny flowers or you cut
mango and melon into stars and scatter them across
the universe that you just created. I can't really
take credit for that idea; it's the way our head chef
from cooking school talked about garnish. But he
was right: cooking is great but it's the big finish in
garnish that makes the dish. It's pretty hard to feel
like Leonardo DaVinci with a slimy chicken breast

under a broiler or a bowl of Romaine and lemon
juice.

I come here to the grocery store every day. I
know my clients' kitchens inside and out. I know
what they have, what they need, what they like.
But still some of them make me grocery lists and it
was sad skittery Mrs. Shane who helped me figure
out why. One day she was watching me and her
maid Maria take everything out of the bags and
put everything away and when I was folding up
the last bag, she said, "where are the children's
chocolate bars?" and I said, "Oh, I think Lucy and
Tyler have chocolate left over from last week" and
she said, "no, I don't think so" and I said, "oh, did
you check?" because I had just checked the day
before and there were two whole bars left and then
she said in this high panicky voice, "no, no, I didn't
check. Why would I check? I don't even know
where Lucy and Tyler keep their chocolate. That's
your job" and then she said she had a headache
and was going upstairs to take a nap. Caffeine
withdrawl, I guess, or else she needed to sleep so
she could forget I didn't bring the chocolate. You
learn a lot about people in this business.

Chocolate really isn't my thing. I'm a salt and
fat kind of person. I can eat a whole bargain size
bag of potato chips and a carton of onion dip while
I watch the 11:00 news. It's hot in Miami and most
of the women here are real skinny and wear hardly
any clothes but I keep the pounds on and wear a lot
of clothes because I keep my apartment really cold
and like it that way. I was never skinny but while I

was in chef school, I had to taste everything I made and you know when your mouth is full of cream and butter all day, it's hard to look like a super model. And now when I get home and it comes time for me to eat, the last thing in the world I want to do is cook. So I eat chips and dip or frozen pizza or sometimes I splurge and go to McDonalds. I know it sounds crazy but when you cook all day like I do, sometimes your tastes change.

So I'm stuck with who I am but it's ok. I don't think anyone would trust a skinny chef, anyway. And the fish man is chubby. Chubby and nice. He has a good smile. Even on days when he doesn't say he likes my hair, he almost always asks me what I'm making. He's interested. And sometimes he offers up his own ways of making things and there have been some times when I've changed my plan and tried his recipes. They're good. He knows what he's talking about and I'd like to talk more about the things he knows. The fish man is a nice man. His shirts are too tight and the space between all the buttons always pops open so I can see his undershirt but I don't care. I think he's cute. And he wears bow ties but no wedding ring and one of these days, I'm going to invite him over for dinner. I can tell he likes to eat. I like that in a man.

So I get to the fish counter and I'm looking carefully at all the kinds of fish because even though you can put anything into a bouillabaisse, I can't just put anything into Mrs. Wallace's. I have to pick things she'll recognize because she's got this thing going where her husband thinks she makes

all the food. If she's not home when it's time for me
to leave, I have to stick a list of what I made and
what's in it behind the bulletin board by her desk so
she can memorize it before her husband gets home.
And it's a funny thing about bouillabaisses because,
really, it's a peasant fish stew. But Mrs. Wallace
thinks it's the be all and end all of what the chefs
call "haute cuisine" and I can just see her strutting
around the kitchen while she heats it up.

I am looking at squid and knowing Mrs.
Wallace would never know how to explain that
when all of a sudden the buzz cut guy is standing
next to me. He's tapping his fingers on top of the
counter but I'm not going to look at him or tell him
that the fish man will be out in a minute. I'm just
going to stand here and decide if it will be scallops
or scampi today. Or both.

"Where's the yams?" this guy says, or at least
that's what I think I hear. He has a southern accent.

I keep looking straight ahead.

"Yams," he says again and just when I'm about
to give up and return "the hairy eyeball," the fish
man comes swinging out through the swinging
doors.

"Hey, chef, how ya doin'?" he says to me.

He's never called me that before and I like
it. I'm about to answer when the buzz cut starts
waving his hand in front of the fish man's face and
says, "d'yall have yams?"

The fish man does not get rattled. He spends
all day in this store and has to deal with all kinds
of people. That's one place where we're different: I

spend all day alone in other people's kitchens.

"Fresh or canned?" the fish man asks.

"Canned," the guy says.

"Right there in the aisle behind you," the fish man says in his usual cheery tone of voice, "around the middle" and the buzz cut guy turns around and goes right back to where we both had just come from.

"Fresh are better," I say, smiling.

"You got that right, Missy," he says and I like being called Missy, too. "What can I do you for today?"

I tell him that I'm making bouillabaisse for Mrs. Wallace tonight and we wink. Last week there was another fish man here, someone I'd never seen before, and he sold me two lobster tails that had been frozen and then thawed. I was just about at the check-out line when the real fish man found me and handed me a package. He said, "I'm a little worried about those tails. They've been thawed too long, I think, and that guy's new, he didn't know. So here," and he handed me a package, "take these. They're still frozen but they'll be ready by the time you get to where you're going." I was bowled over by how sweet that was. So I thanked him and told him about Mrs. Wallace and her bouillabaisse, how her husband thinks she does all the shopping and all the cooking and how I don't even think he knows I exist. I've never seen him and she pays me in cash. So this time he said, "Let me go in the back and get you some good tails then" and he disappeared back into the swinging doors.

Mrs. Wallace wants the bouillabaisse once a week but on the other days she's grilled chicken or poached salmon all the way. She says her husband doesn't like the sour cream and dill sauce that I make to go with the salmon and she takes that personally. So now I just put lemon wedges on the side. The funny thing is she's not as skinny as she should be if all she's eating is what I make for her, so she must be eating something else when I'm not around. She must be shopping too because Mrs. Wallace's list never has anything on it that isn't low fat and low carb and low cal. Maybe she comes here in a big hat and dark glasses and when I think that, I wonder if I'd recognize her.

But my clients can't fool me. Like Mrs. Morton. Right now in my cart I have cream cheese, butter, sour cream, eggs, brown sugar, and heavy cream because I'm supposed to make her mother a cheesecake for her 80th birthday. And I will. But Mrs. Morton's mother won't eat cheesecake because dairy doesn't agree with her and I know it because every time she comes over for dinner, she hobbles into the kitchen on thin bones that could use some dairy and says to me, "Darlene, you're not putting no dairy in that dinner, are you? I can't have no dairy" and I say no, of course I'm not. Mrs. Morton's mother talks as if she's never been to school, which is odd because Mrs. Morton talks like she's the Queen of England and sometimes I wonder what Mrs. Morton was like when she was a kid, though she doesn't seem like she could ever have been one.

The fish man comes back out but he doesn't just have the lobster tails. He also has scallops and shrimps, all pink and shiny, a net bag of tiny clams and a big piece of cod. He remembers what I buy for my bouillabaisse.

"I know old Mrs. Wallace wouldn't recognize mussels," he says, holding up the bag of clams, and we have a laugh. Then the most amazing thing happens. He says, "I bet Mrs. Wallace's bouillabaisse is really good" and I say "it's the best" because, really, it is and he says "I wish I could try it" and I say "well, you know? If you give me double of what you're giving me now, I could make an extra batch and you could come over for dinner" and he says "really?" and I say "sure" and he says "ok then, great" and goes back into the back for double of everything. It all happens so fast. One minute I'm looking at scallops and the next minute, I have a date with the fish man.

When he comes back out and hands me the packages, I hand him my card. He sees the address and says, "this is where you live?" and I'm feeling giddy so I say "well, why don't you come and find out?" because I guess I'm flirting now too and he says "what time?" and I say, "8:00" and he says "see you then" and I say "you bet." I'm done with my shopping but I hurry back to the dairy aisle to get double of what's already in my cart because if I can make one cheesecake, I can make two and me and the fish man will need some dessert. I stop in the wine aisle and know just what I need, sauvignon blanc. We had to take a wine course in chef school. At the time, I thought it was kind of boring but now I'm so happy I know what kind of wine is best with spicy fish stew. My heart is dancing around in my chest. The fish man is coming over for dinner. I don't even know his name.

The grocery store is very crowded at this hour and I try to figure out which line will be the fastest. I have to go home and make two cheesecakes. Then I have to deliver Mrs. Morton's and then head over to Mrs. Wallace's to make her bouillabaisse and then rush back home to make an even better batch for tonight. I pick a line that I think will go fast because the cashier is RoseLauree and she's young and spunky and usually whips the items over the scanner in no time. While I'm waiting, I think about what I'm going to wear.

None of my clothes are really fit for a date—I either have chef's clothes or sweatshirts and pants that match. I have a few good things but they're too good for a first dinner date, a long black velvet skirt I wear when I cater at Christmas and a sparkly top for New Year's Eve. I have a lot of t-shirts but none of them are nice enough. Today I'm wearing one of my favorite ones that says "Cleveland Browns" on the front. I love the Cleveland Browns—they're scrappy and they're almost always the underdogs but they have vision and they have faith and one day I just know they'll win the Super Bowl. You gotta believe. It's only July so football won't start up again for a while but I like to get a jump on things. But I can't wear this tonight. So I take a mental tour of my closet while I wait for

RoseLauree to ring up the three people in front of
me and while I'm on that tour, I see some things I
had forgotten about that I don't necessarily want to
see.

One time when I was leaving Mrs. Conway's
house, she came stumbling into the kitchen carrying
a box that was so big I couldn't even see her
head behind it. She was out of breath and saying,
"Darlene, Darlene, wait, hang on" and I did, of
course. She set the box down on the island and
said, "here are some things I thought you might
like." It was an old box that had been closed up
with fat strips of silver duct tape so I knew it wasn't
a present. When I didn't say anything, because I
really didn't know what to say, she said, "do we
have a knife?" A lot of my clients don't even know
what's in their kitchens and if I was a different kind
of person, I could take whatever I wanted and they
would never know it. The Conways have the best
knives money can buy so I went to where I keep
their Wüsthofs and thought I'd better just give her
something small, like the paring knife, so she could
open the box without hurting herself. Wüsthofs
are very sharp and dangerous if you're not used
to using knives. I thought they'd be especially
dangerous for a person who didn't even know she
had any knives so I decided just to cut through the
duct tape myself.

Mrs. Conway has two daughters and they are
both in college. Colleen is a senior at Cornell and
she loves to ski. Inside the box were old ski pants,
two knit caps, a big fisherman's knit sweater and

a puffy down jacket that took up a lot of space. I thought, oh, these will be very useful for a big girl like me here in Miami but I just looked at them and then tried to smile. The other daughter is Constance and according to Mrs. Conway, she could have gotten into any college she wanted but she chose University of Miami because she wanted to study marine biology and be on the water all the time, too. There were some bathing suits in the box that must have belonged to Constance. Maybe she got tired of them.

The girls are only a year apart and so Mrs. Conway had it arranged that they would have their coming out parties at the same time. That year I made more money in a week than I sometimes make in three months because the Conways had a party every night the week before the debutante ball. Colleen and Constance wore a different ball gown to every party we gave and all the ball gowns were in the box, too.

Mrs. Conway was smiling at me in that way that said she thought she was doing the greatest thing anyone had ever done for me. I wanted to suggest she give these things to Goodwill, or even to tell her that she was giving that term a new meaning but instead I picked the box up. I really thought I was going to say thank you but then found that I couldn't get it to come out of my mouth. Mrs. Conway didn't understand what was going on in my head. She said, "Darlene, no, really, don't worry about it. These are things I want you to have. Honestly." But the problem wasn't that I didn't believe her. It was that I had been working for her for five years and she had never seen me.

All those ski clothes and bikinis and ball gowns are folded neatly on the floor in my closet next to my shoes. I'm not sure why they're still there except you never know what could happen. It's like life and cooking and the Cleveland Browns. You gotta believe.

RoseLauree looks up from ringing up items of the person two in front of me and winks. "Heya Darling," she says and I don't know if it's because she doesn't know my name or thinks it's "Darling" instead of "Darlene" or just wants to call me Darling but I have never cared. "Hi RoseLauree," I say and I could just call her Rose—we know each other that well—but I love her whole name and the way it sounds. When I say it, she rolls her eyes and smiles. We see each other every day; even when I don't go in her line, I always stop by and say hi to her on my way out. I'm older than she is and there's also a lot of other differences between us—she from Haiti and I'm from here, she's a vegetarian and I love my meat, she's already been married twice and I've never even been married once but tonight I have a date with the fish man and I can't wait to tell her. "Hurry" I mouth to her and she nods her head but then rolls her eyes again because the woman she's waiting on is examining a huge stack of coupons she's just pulled out of her purse. I shrug my shoulders and me and RoseLauree have a good silent laugh.

I'm thinking about what's in my closet again

that I could actually wear and I decide on a pair
on black stretch pants and the blue denim shirt I
bought last year when I took myself to the Miami
Seaquarium. I really wanted to see the dolphins.
They were adorable. I bought the shirt because it
has a dolphin stitched onto the front pocket. It's
blue and my eyes are blue and I have some blue
sparkly hair clips that I can wear too. If I ever get
out of this grocery store, I might even have time
to heat up my old rollers and curl my hair a little
bit. When I was in chef school, the school secretary
was my good friend. Her name was Paola and she
had thirteen grandchildren. There were pictures of
them all over her desk. Some of them lived here in
Miami but most of them lived in Peru. Paola used
to always tell me stories about them. She also used
to always tell me that I had beautiful blue eyes
and that if I lost some weight, I'd be very pretty.
I loved Paola but I never knew how to feel about
that because you have the looks you're born with
whether you should lose some weight or not. I have
good skin and no wrinkles and I sometimes think
it's because I don't worry a lot about the things I
see other people worrying about. Still, I'm a little
worried at the moment because I need to go. I want
to be very pretty tonight.

    Finally, there is only one more person in front
of me. I am next in line. I look at my watch and
realize that way more time has gone by than I
thought and I am going to have to hustle to get
everything done. RoseLauree is her usual happy
easy self. She is Colleen and Constance's age but

that's where that comparison ends. They are good girls and nice but nervous and fidgety all of the time. RoseLauree doesn't have half what they have but she has a price scanner that makes her job easier, a stool to sit on, some water to sip from and not a care in the world. While I'm waiting now, I look at the magazines in the rack next to me and then I pick up two packages of TicTacs so my breath will be good tonight. You never know what might happen, especially after a couple glasses of sauvignon blanc. Just then, I feel someone tapping me on the shoulder. It's the buzz cut guy. He has two cans of yams.

"Scuse me, maam, but seeing as I only have these cans of yams and I'm in a hurry, can I go in front of you?"

Well, we're both in a hurry so we have that in common but "Maam" certainly sets us apart. Normally it would make me feel like an old hobbly grandmother but I'm too happy to be mad. And even if I was mad, I would probably have said yes since he did only have two cans of yams and I had double of everything in my cart but I have to go and I don't know what will happen if I try to get into another line. It's been such a long time since I was in a hurry. I shop slowly and drive slowly and cook food very slowly because I always want it to be perfect for my customers and I never have anywhere I'm supposed to be at any special time. But today is different. So I shake my head to say no and I'm about to say I'm sorry but I'm in a hurry today and have been waiting in this line a long time. I'm also about to tell him that just over there is a line for ten items or less and he'd get through that line quick but before I have a chance to say any of that, he says, "stupid cow" and slams the cans down on the conveyer. He's tapping his fingers on top of one can.

I turn my back to him and will RoseLauree to hurry up. My hackles are up, as they say. I don't know why people can do that, ask you a question and then be so rude if you don't give them the answer they want. When Mrs. Conway put all the clothes her daughters didn't need anymore and that I would never need back into the box and I lifted it and was walking out the door, she said in a voice that made me nervous, "you're welcome" because I hadn't been able to get the thank you that was in my head to come out of my mouth. Those words probably didn't know where to go because they didn't know what to thank her for. So I suppose this guy calling me a "cow" is sort of the same thing; he thinks he has the right because I didn't give the answer he expected me to give.

But something else is not right. He's too angry and too nervous. I see it now but realize I sensed it before, in the canned goods aisle and at the fish counter. And he just has two cans of yams. If he was a grandmother or if he was a person with a cart full of things that go with yams, like greens and onions, a ham or a turkey or even marshmallows, I would understand it better but here's a young skinny guy with a buzzcut who had to be told where canned yams were. I am feeling nervous. He must be on drugs.

"Move it," he says to me the next minute, when RoseLauree is almost done with the customer in front of me and there is some space between my groceries and hers.

"Why don't you go into that express line?" I say to him, turning my head just slightly over my shoulder to speak to him and pointing to the fast lane.

"Why don't you just mind your own business?" he says in return, and then he pushed his two cans of yams into the plastic bar separating my groceries from his. Someone has just gotten in line behind him and is piling groceries onto the conveyer belt behind his yams. Now we are both trapped.

"Hurry it up, RoseLauree," I say and I try to say it in my most upbeat kidding-around voice, so she won't get mad but also so that she will hurry it up. First she looks up at me, maybe to give me our usual shrug, but then she sees the buzzcut guy behind me and her face freezes and her shoulders raise and it looks like she has stopped breathing. Suddenly I realize why he is in this long line.

RoseLauree has told me about so many of her lovers, so many boyfriends and the two husbands that I have no idea which one this guy is but I know he is one of them. She sees him and then immediately looks back to her cash register. I hear him say "shit" and then hear him tapping his fingers louder. "Nice job," he says I think to me because he must have wanted to take her by surprise. But it's obvious RoseLauree doesn't want to see him and then I see her looking around the store, like maybe she thinks she needs some help.

There is a group of three store managers clustered at the end of the check-out aisle next to us. Because I come here every day and have for so many years, I know all their names: one is Mario, one is Ray and one is called Dak. Dak is my favorite; if I was a cute skinny girl, he'd be the person at the grocery store I'd have a crush on because he is very nice and very handsome. And he always helps me when I need something special. I know he would help now if he knew me and RoseLauree were in trouble but he doesn't have a clue. Right now, he is stepping backward a little, putting his feet apart and his hands together between his legs and then raising those clasped hands in the air and I know he is telling Mario and Ray a story about his golf game. Once he told me about a golf game and so I know it will be a long time before any of them looks up at me or RoseLauree.

And she knows it too.

But then it is my turn. RoseLauree starts scanning my items but not in her usual way. She is doing it really slowly, too slowly, and she keeps looking at me and then up over my head to the managers who are talking about golf and then back to me and then to my groceries. All along, I wanted to tell her about my date with the fish man, maybe even ask her if she can tell me his name, but now I just want to ask her what I should do. Who is this guy? What is going on? What could happen?

The guy bagging my groceries is Slow
Willie. He's in his sixties and he's worked
at this store for over twenty years. He says
"paperorplasticpaperorplasticpaperorplastic" every
single day and won't stop saying it until you pick
one. No matter who you are or how often you
come here. Every time I always say "plastic" even
though he always asks it while he's already started
putting my groceries in paper bags and normally
I don't care because he's sweet and slow and it
doesn't matter but today it seems to matter more
than anything. Today I think he should recognize
me, see who I am, know I want plastic.

"Plastic, Willie," I say, too loud, loud enough
for the buzzcut guy to get annoyed and start hissing
at me like a vampire but not loud enough for any
of the managers to even look up.

"RoseLauree," I say, "I don't know what to do."

But RoseLauree doesn't answer. She scans the
groceries, Willie puts them in the bags. Mario
laughs and slaps Dak on the back and then they
all start laughing. In some ways, everything is
like it is all the time except that time is moving
too quickly and too slowly all at once and I don't
know what will happen when Slow Willie asks if
he can help me carry my groceries to the car and I
say no thank you like I always do because I'm in
such a hurry and because I want someone to be
here with RoseLauree because I don't know what
this guy will do when his two cans of yams get to
her scanner and she has to look him in the eye but
I also don't know what I would do if I stayed or

what I will do when I go and I've finished doing all
the things I've known how to do for such a long
time and am then looking at myself in the mirror, in
my dolphin shirt, waiting for a man whose name I
don't know to come over to my house for dinner.